COZY CABINS AND FERRY TALES

A GREENSEA ISLAND ADVENTURE

BOOK 2

JULIE FARLEY

FOG HOUSE
PRESS

To my favorites...

GREENSEA GAZETTE

Islanders,

Happy almost fall! Retire the white and get out the flannel. It's the last weekend of summer! What a summer it's been thanks to Johnny Nickel's hit song, "Greensea Gal." We sure hope Johnny and Jac pop over to the island to say hi sometime this fall. Until then, say good riddance to all the summer residents and hello to the big yellow buses. Local season is back! Congratulations, we made it through another summer!

The cougar is on the prowl, and I'm not looking at you and your animal print outfits, Laura Prescott. Last night, someone caught the real animal on camera sniffing around Bungalow Bay, and this morning there was plenty of scat lying around in the Grand Green Forest. You know the drill: keep a close eye on small pets and children. I think we're all still mourning the death of Mr. Pickles, the pet bunny who wandered around Gulls Point last year after his dad errantly left the cage open overnight, leaving Mr. Pickles to fall victim to a ravenous cougar.

Since we're entering fall, all eyes are on Applehill Farm, awaiting the heir apparent. If they don't arrive, what will happen to Harvest Fest? And what if they arrive and they want nothing to do with the festival? Don started Harvest Fest to give something back to the community he loved so much. Be ready to step in, Islanders. Nothing is more important than the survival of the festival and Don's legacy.

Keep it real out there, folks. The countdown to school is on!

XOXO,

GG

ONE

Goodbye to the creeps who stuffed the paddle boards with sand, the tourists who glued the oars together, and the foodies who ordered way too many marionberry pies. Hello, full-time Greensea residents! We're at the start of islander season, my favorite time of year! If I didn't have to work three jobs today, I'd crack open a celebratory beer. Instead, in between surveying apple trees, I'm composing an email to the heir of Applehill Farm.

To: sdp@email.com
From: jmatey@email.com
Subj: Awaiting Your Arrival

Ms. DuPont,

Ms. DuPont? The name sounds like a pedigree.

I am currently undertaking the care of your uncle's property. I cannot continue to care for it while I continue my other, more pressing, responsibilities. Please advise when you will arrive to relieve me of my duties.

Sincerely,
J. Sherman

Don't get me wrong. I've been happy to help with Applehill Farm after Don's untimely death, but taking over the care of such an enormous property and the upcoming event is beyond my mental capacity at the moment.

Applehill Farm is a five-acre piece of land with a long gravel driveway lined with, you guessed it, apple trees. A log cabin sits at the bottom of the property on the edge of a cove off of Bungalow Bay. A barn, almost as big as the cabin, sits at the top of the property. I'm not a farmer, and I know very little about caring for trees bearing fruit. Or things that lay eggs. Or barns. Or large pieces of property. I live in a studio apartment above the family store.

Harvest Fest at Applehill Farm is one of Greensea's favorite traditions. It has the pageantry of Groundhog Day, the fun of an Easter Egg Hunt, and the excitement of a hot dog eating contest. Not having it would be tantamount to canceling Christmas. We owe it to Don's legacy to make it better than ever. Hence the reason I need the heir to arrive stat.

My pocket buzzes. Every time my phone rings I cringe,

because I'm afraid each call will somehow add to my to-do list. But this time, it's Jac.

"Sorry I couldn't make it to the big meeting of the parents, sis." It was an important weekend for my sister and her boyfriend, Johnny Nickel. Our parents met his mom in London after a concert. By all accounts, it was a smashing success.

"I know you're busy holding down everyone's fort on Greensea, bro," says Jac. "You need to take your life off the back burner, even though it's good to get your nose out of those enormous books."

Besides my apple duties, I'm taking care of the family store, Cedar & Fern, while Mom and Dad are on their never-ending trip to Europe.

"I will. With any luck, the person who inherited this place will turn up soon." I pick apples and place them in a bucket.

"Josh, you're a good person to take up all that work at the farm."

"Blah, blah, blah." I'm just a person who ended up in the wrong place at the wrong time—Maya, Don's longtime girlfriend, standing there crying about losing Don; the lawyer explaining the next-of-kin situation; all while I was trying to finish up the map of the property for Harvest Fest. One thing led to another, and here we are. "Maybe Mom and Dad will turn up and take care of Cedar & Fern."

"Don't bet on that. They're pretty happy tearing it up around Europe. They're giggly and acting like teenagers," says Jac.

"Gross." That's the last thing I want to hear. It's my turn to seek new pastures beyond the horizon of Greensea. "Someday my time will come."

"Did you hear the new song?" asks Jac. Now she's the one who sounds like a giggly teenager.

"Sure did. You're famous. Your name is etched into the annals of history."

"Haha. Tell that to my first grade students."

"Gotta go, sis. My to-do list is calling my name. Tell that rockstar to behave and I'll see you soon."

Okay. Job one at the orchard done. Next stop—fix the broken fridge at Cedar & Fern.

Cedar & Fern resembles a ragtag fishing village: three clapboard buildings painted in various shades of green. Even in my Prius, kicking up a few rocks and following the ridiculously low island speed limits, it only takes me seven minutes to get there from the farm. Got to love the fact that nothing is too far away on this itty bitty island.

The wood floors are uneven and worn, but doing the job. The doors creak and the windows whistle. It's the bane of my existence and as familiar as my big toe.

The staff moved everything over to the refrigerator in the other building, so it's lunch in my apartment while I text a repairman. Bean and bacon soup and five minutes with *The New Yorker*. Peace, until my phone pings with a reply from the heir.

Hi, Mr. Sherman!

Thank you so much for taking care of everything. I'm tying up loose ends on the East Coast and will start the trip out there in the next few days. It is quite a journey, so I can't give you an exact date of my arrival. I plan to drive to Pittsburgh, and then onto Chicago. I've never been that far west before, so there will be a lot to see. After trying some

deep-dish pizza (Giordano's or Gino's East?) it will be on to Minneapolis. And then some city in North Dakota, or is it South Dakota? On to Montana, with maybe a quick stop down in Yellowstone because my gosh, how many times in your life do you drive past that? Do you think bison are actually just off the side of the road? Missoula next, then Spokane, and then on to Seattle for the ferryboat to Greensea Island. I'd say the trip will take over a week to ten days as long as Old Blue keeps chugging. Can't wait to meet you!

S.

Mother of all things that are holy! I just wanted to know when she was going to arrive, not a litany of what she wants to do on the trip. I'm surprised she didn't include bathroom breaks.

Ms. DuPont,

I will leave a key under the mat for your eventual arrival.

J. Sherman

I don't have time to play tour guide to this one. If I'm not careful, I'll end up mapping out her days on Greensea.

Hi Again!

Thank you so much! Do you think that's safe? No one will steal my uncle's things, will they? I'd hate to have anything happen to his house before I get there. Is it actually a farm? Like, are there fields and a barn? I don't know very much about caring for 5.48 acres, such a large piece of property. Will there be someone to teach me how to care for everything on my own? I've read *Farming for Dummies* and I'm doing as much research as I can on the history of the island. I want to preserve Uncle Don's memory as best as I can. So appreciate any help.

S.

Ms. DuPont,

Greensea is a very safe island. The last thing that was stolen was Mrs. Dunlap's blueberry pie in 1975, and it turned out her neighbor's horse stole it. There will be people for you to reach out to, but you will mainly work on the farm on your own.

J.

I'm thirty freaking years old sitting in a small apartment above my parents' store, eating soup from a can. My social life consists of talking to an occasional yammering non-islander and people coming in to pick up their weekly milk order. I need a change. I need something bigger.

TWO

SYLVIANE

It's Friday the 13th. A full moon. Mercury is in retrograde. And my luck has changed.

"I can't believe Uncle Don left me his farm." I look at Dad as I read the email from the caretaker again.

"Well, he loved you." Dad sets his reading glasses on his desk. "And it's what your mom would have wanted."

Applehill Farm on Honeysuckle Lane. On a place called Greensea Island. On the opposite coast, 3,000 miles away from Virginia. Fairy tales are made of this kind of stuff.

"I'll miss you," I sigh as I rub my lucky citrine necklace.

"Oh, sweetie, I'll miss you too, but Nancy and I will visit soon, and this is what you were meant to do." Dad glances at his laptop. He said he was working, but the reflection in the window lets me know he's reading the sports page.

I would love for my dad to visit, but Nancy? No thanks.

"Sylviane." A voice from the kitchen breaks me away from my thoughts. "It's time."

My dad looks at me. "It's nice of you to perform at Parker's birthday party today."

I'd do anything for that little pipsqueak, even if his mom and grandma aren't my biggest fans. Nancy's never impressed with anything that has to do with me, the unlucky girl without a mother. Sometimes I think the Brothers Grimm wrote my life story. Mother died in childbirth. Father married an evil woman with a golden child. In pictures we look like the Brady Bunch, but in real life we're more like a modern-day *Cinderella*.

"He loves my magic tricks," I answer, which is why Nancy offered to pay me for this gig.

Becoming a part-time magician had seemed like a romantic, very Charles Dickens-esque way to support myself after college, while I pursued my dream of a byline above the fold. I imagined red curtains, velvet capes, and black top hats. Steampunk outfits mixed with Cirque du Soleil-style illusions. A side hustle ending with my name in lights. Until I started doing the job. And my deck of cards fell into a dish of salsa during my Wednesday night gig at La Casita. Or my magic wand ended up covered in leftover buttercream frosting at the birthday party du jour. The paycheck from either barely covered my gas money. The reality of being a part-time magician at almost thirty, with my name far below the fold, is more Amelia Bedelia than great literature.

I make my way out to the backyard, where an inflatable bouncy house sits in one of the far corners. A pony, with a teenage guide paying more attention to her phone than the animal, relieves itself near the plastic kiddie pool. A clown is setting up a face-painting station. An organic cotton candy machine roars to life next to the bouncy house. (Is organic cotton candy a thing, or has some sly creator stuck the word in front of the same cotton candy they had at the county fair?) A piñata in the shape of a shark hangs from a pole. And a picnic table, with bags and bags of snacks, waits for hungry party goers. In the center of the yard sits a circular table covered in a blue checkered tablecloth. A dozen little red cups with ping-pong balls sit on the table, positioned for the win-a-goldfish game. This party has all the things.

And it takes two seconds to remember why I'm dreading this job even though my nephew's dimply smile cuts straight to my heart. Nancy is standing with her hands on her hips, her perfect bob still in the breeze.

"Magician," says Nancy. "I don't want anything to upset Parker's birthday party. Are your pants blue or black?" She straightens the starched pleats of her own cranberry-red pants.

"Black. That's what you requested." But shit. The tag at Goodwill hadn't specified the color—I might be wrong. Just as long as Nancy doesn't get any closer to inspect them and notice the masking tape I used to hem them.

"Just making sure. And I hope you spice your tricks up a bit. None of the dribble I saw at the Mexican restaurant last month."

"No problem, Nancy. You will get your money's worth."

Unfortunately, the act I planned is the same one I did at La Casita on the first Wednesday of the month. Nancy may not have been impressed with that act, but Parker thought my card tricks were top tier. I can't abracadabra myself out of this situation, so I'd better get my butt in gear and try to wow some kids while I pull Tabatha, the magic rabbit, out of the hat.

"A nervous magician is not a believable magician," scolds Nancy, watching me fix my flyaways and lick my already chapped lips.

"Where would you like me?" I ask, looking around for quick escape routes just in case.

"Over there, Sylviane." Nancy points across the yard to a card table leaning against the fence.

On my way to the designated spot, I see Parker and give him a quick birthday hug.

"Thanks, Sylvan and Tabatha," he says in his squeaky little kid voice. He's the only person I don't correct when he mispronounces my name. One day he'll stop saying things like rainbrellas and actually pronounce my name perfectly, Sil-vee-ann, but today is for celebrating him and not correcting.

I pull Tabatha around a little patch of grass, hoping she'll take care of her business before I get my show underway. But Tabatha, the rabbit born under a Taurus moon, is in a stubborn mood, and the noise and the heat of the day will not make her any more agreeable. I peek down at my armpits to see if I have sweat stains before Nancy can point them out. I cover the table with a purple velvet tablecloth and set out my tricks: a pile of playing cards to show off my card-guessing skills, a plain old balloon ready to turn into an animal of the child's choice, a wand possessing secret flowers, and a top hat that would house the magical rabbit. I murmur the Roald Dahl quote I sewed into my bag of tricks, "Those who don't believe in magic will never find it." And add, "Make them believe." The words are my superhero pose and the first thing I ever do before performing.

"If that rabbit is part of your act, you'd better hide it." Nancy points to Tabatha. Nancy's demonstrative index finger is her signature pose. I give the rabbit a tug.

"This is Parker's sixth birthday. I will not stand for an obstinate rabbit messing anything up."

"Yes, I know how important this party is to you." Every social gathering, from a mid-morning coffee to Friday night bunco, is of the utmost importance to Nancy.

The kids start to arrive and place their gifts on a table near the entrance to the backyard, and my first customers gather around the table as I attempt to pull my rabbit out of the hat. But today, Tabatha feels like she may have eaten a Rottweiler.

She doesn't budge. I say, "Abracadabra," over and over as the kids sit criss-cross applesauce in front of me. And nothing happens. I add an alla kazaam to the abracadabra, and still no rabbit.

"Please, Tabatha, not now," I whisper. I try again. And again. And after what feels like seventeen tries, Tabatha appears, but most of the kids have already run off for snacks or face painting. I hear a party go-er complaining about the trick, so I'm not surprised when I see Nancy and her kitten heels coming my way.

"Daydreaming, Magician?" Nancy snarls from the side of the bouncy house. As usual, I'm her only focus today.

"No, just waiting for some more customers. I think they might be a little bored with the flowers at the end of the wand and the rabbit in my hat." Crap. My fatal flaw, being honest in everything I say, plays right into Nancy's hand again.

"It's your style. They're bored with your presentation. That little boy just ran over and told me you couldn't pull the rabbit out of the hat. How is that even possible? Give it a little pizazz and they'll be lining up across the yard. Pretend you like it here. I am paying you, after all."

Yes, I'm being paid. I think for a second. I know one trick that's guaranteed to be a showstopper. Not of the sawing a child in half variety, but something that would make them all gasp, and that would be sure to make Parker giggle. If it went right or wrong. It's a risk, but nothing is going to redeem me in Nancy's eyes anyway. So there's nothing to lose, except my pay, which, honestly, is barely enough to make me think twice.

"Hold on to your horses," I whisper.

I put my fingers to my mouth and let out a whistle louder than any of the pretend-to-be-sweet voices the moms have ever used. The whistle stops everyone in their tracks. They stop bouncing, riding, and eating. The clown stops painting faces, and the pony stands still. Even the mommies clucking in the corner stop to look.

I take a deep breath, muster up all of my confidence, and get ready for my show-stopping idea. I stand next to a party table clad with the goldfish game. Underneath the cups is the canvas blue checkered tablecloth. Without giving it any more thought, I grab one end of the tablecloth.

"O.K., guys. I need you to count to three with me and then say ABRACADABRA!"

The kids oblige, and the moms are afraid to utter a peep.

"ONE...TWO...THREE...ABRACADABRA!"

On abracadabra, I give the tablecloth one big pull. I'm doing the old party trick I've watched my dad, much to Nancy's chagrin, do year after year. The kids gasp. One little girl gives a scream.

Nancy yells, "NOOOOOOO!"

And voila, out comes the tablecloth, game still intact, and the fish, sitting next to the table out of harm's way, don't even bat an eye. Everyone claps. I rub my gemstone necklace and say a quiet "thank you" to myself.

"Was that enough style?" I ask Nancy, who is frozen with her mouth open next to my stepsister and the rest of the moms.

"Yeah, yeah, that was good. Thanks for teaching the kids a party trick they can't try at home. You could have made quite a mess. What were you thinking, Sylviane?" Nancy asks.

"I'm a magician. You hired me to bring the magic, and that's just what I did." I rub the jade crystal I have hidden in the pocket of my maybe-black pants for good luck.

"Well, I know I can do a lot of things, but I still don't do them."

A towering frosted cake, three layers high, set on fire by skinny curlicue candles, arrives and changes the subject. I pack my bag with all of my props and the can-do attitude I earned.

Tabatha tries to run away from her life in the top hat, but I retrieve her with no one looking away from the cake.

"Oh, did you see the pictures of the engagement ring? Just stunning!" exclaims Nancy, as I head for the exit.

Straight to the heart.

"Yes, Nancy. I got your text with all the pictures of the proposal."

Ryder, my kind of sort of boyfriend of a few years, proposed to his regal French girlfriend. So that's the other reason she wanted me to work the party. More time to remind me, before I leave, of the love I'll never have. And she knows love is the thing I want more than anything. The thing I've always pined after. I love boyfriends, flowers, meet cutes. Straining for a little glimpse, catching a sniff of something that reminds you of the one who has your heart. I love love. And I don't have it, apparently never have had it, and I won't get it from Ryder. Something Nancy is thrilled to remind me, even though she would love nothing more than to call Ryder's family in-laws.

Years ago, I would've traded all the money in the world for his love. Now, I'm just ready to stop feeling like his old, comfortable pair of jeans you can't throw out. And I finally have a way to do it. Ryder's been my slot machine. I can't stop putting in my quarters, hoping, against the odds, that I'll hit the jackpot one of these times. Instead, I get the tiny payouts and never all the bells and whistles. Since he put a ring on the other girl's finger, it's time for some closure. Maybe love is on the other coast. Maybe this full moon is a harbinger of good things to come.

"Bye, Nancy. I leave for Greensea Island tomorrow," I say.

Nancy looks at me and says, "You know, you've always lacked gumption. Never had any get up and go. Didn't want to take the extra ballet class with Caroline when we first met. You got a B on that French project in seventh grade and never did that extra credit. You never wanted to earn all the Girl Scout badges. The hardest thing to parent is a child with no initiative." She looks at me with her steely blue eyes. "We'll see if you make it all the way out to Greensea or stop and give up in Iowa or something."

Nice. My lack of initiative at age four, as a motherless child, is to blame for Nancy's inability to act with any empathy or sympathy for the last twenty-five years.

"No worries, Nancy. You've given me all the gumption I need to make this journey."

Because I'm Sylviane of the forest. My name is my crown jewel, a built-in conversation starter, and the future that's been written in my palm. I've got this new beginning.

THREE

SYLVIANE

Hello!

I should be on the island in the next few days! Barring any super exciting attractions I see on the side of the road. I saw a moose in Wyoming, and I'm still pinching myself. I just had to explore the ghost town in Montana, which added a few extra hours, because who knows when I'll be that close to one again? It was just like being on the set of a movie. I read that there's a waterfall after I get through the Cascades—by the way, the pass scares me. Are there cliffs on either side as I drive through the mountain? I'm trying to decide if I want to stop or not. If I don't, I'll be there sooner rather than later!

Thanks again for taking care of my uncle's property! It means so much to me.

S.

The caretaker sounds like an old curmudgeon, but he's probably dealing with his own grief after Uncle Don's passing. The farm must be a constant reminder to him that Don's left. I'll make it my mission to brighten his day as soon as I arrive. Until then, my email update will have to suffice.

So many exits off the highway look the same. Gigantic gas stations offering showers for truckers and snacks for weary drivers. Fast-food hamburger joints. If you're lucky, a coffee joint. I eat one meal a day in the car and one meal a day in a vinyl booth at one of the fast-food spots. I alternate between breakfast and lunch. For dinner, I try to look a few miles beyond the Hampton Inn of choice. Sometimes, it's a local pizza place with fairy lights hanging from the ceiling. Other times, it's a diner with jukeboxes at each booth. Each hotel looks the same. A double bed, white bedding, nightstand with a bible in the top drawer. Rosemary shampoo and conditioner in the shower, along with a complementary bottle of body wash. The tufted beige carpet feels the same in each state.

The big difference is the landscape. The farther west I drive, the bigger the landscape gets. It goes from vast fields to rolling hills to mountains bigger than I've seen before. I wonder what made people settle in each of the cities. Were they just too tired to go on? Or did they think there was nothing beyond what they found?

I pull a quote from my purple velvet messenger bag, "Not all those who wander are lost." Thanks to the great Tolkien. And that's why I stop at every random attraction that appeals to me. I'm not lost. I'm learning. I'm living. It gives me a picture different from the monotony or the typical roadside exit. It also gives me more reason to keep on chugging. On Old Blue's dashboard, I keep my mom's yellow-edged photo of the cabin by the bay . It is my light at the end of the tunnel. The pot of gold at the end of the rainbow. I have to keep going to get to the place she'd dreamed about.

The key is STILL under the mat waiting for you.

J.

Thanks, Mr. Grumpy Pants. Operation Make Him Cheerful shall begin shortly.

———

Officially ten days and 2,867 miles after the birthday party, I pull onto a ferryboat, heading to Uncle Don's cabin on Greensea Island, searching for my true happily ever after. As I stand on the car deck of the ferry, seagulls fly by with leftover fried clams in their beaks. Ferry horns blast shallow warnings to other boats. And the damp salty air kisses my cheeks as the boat leaves the shore.

"Ferry hair don't care!" I whisper into the breeze as the wind takes my blonde bob in seven different directions.

"Be careful over there," an older gentleman says as he passes by. I smile, because nothing can happen while I'm standing here on the floor of this overflowing, floating parking garage with a four-foot steel wall protecting us from a cold emerald sea, but I appreciate his care.

I tuck my hands into the sleeves of last year's Christmas present from my dad. A stiff gray water-repellent raincoat, expensive enough to force satisfaction and generic enough to still leave me cold. I peer over the edge to get a better view of the city, just as a seagull dives and relieves itself on my head.

Shiiiit. Literally. I see the slimy goo falling down my shirt and my favorite jeans that already needed to be washed. I grab one of a dozen fast-food napkins out of my lucky messenger bag and try to wipe the crap out of my hair, which is more difficult because my hair's grown bigger in the sea air. I just hope there's truth to the old wives' tale that bird poop is a sign of hope, and not my regular old bad luck traveling across the Puget Sound with me. For the first time in forever, I cannot wait to do laundry.

I'm a mess, but I need to go get some of the clam chowder I read about in the guidebook to Seattle that I memorized each night in unfamiliar hotel rooms across the country. I'm a walking encyclopedia of activities in the Greater Seattle area, and ferry chowder is the first item on my ever-growing bucket list.

The ferry safety announcement echoes gently in the background as I walk across the long car deck following the signs to the passenger deck. "Welcome to the Washington State Ferry system..." My ears perk up and listen to the rules of the boat as I walk up the stairs. No unattended bags or children. No running. No flash photography. I wish they'd add, for the teenagers I can see out of the corner of my eye, no reenacting the iconic moment in *Titanic*.

People with a clear idea of where they're going hurry by me. My legs are happy to have the opportunity to climb two flights of steps after sitting in the car for so many days. I follow the signs to the galley, passing booth after booth filled with people. The cafeteria is bigger, and way more gourmet, than I expected. Local beers, wines, personal veggie and cheese trays, Greek yogurt parfaits, smothered tater tots, and cups of organic ice cream line the respective hot and cold shelves. The smell of freshly popped popcorn wins the battle with the sea air. This is nothing like the rest stops I've visited for the last thousand miles on I-90.

I grab a cup of chowder and get in line. The tater tots catch my eye, so I set my soup down and reach for some. And, oh my gosh, that pretzel looks ah-mazing. Add that to my pile.

I hear a book slam closed behind me, so I turn around to see a guy in a leather jacket standing there with a hefty copy of *The Complete Works of Charles Dickens*. His outfit feels like he should be reading *Zen and the Art of Motorcycle Maintenance* instead of an old English author.

"Can I help you, Oliver Twist?" I ask, proud and surprised by my quick Dickens reference.

"Just thought you might want to check out before the boat docks. The crossing is only thirty-two minutes long," says the stranger with dark brown eyes, bushy eyebrows, and a sideways smirk—half smile, half grimace, all smolder.

"Cat got your tongue, Miss Havisham?" he asks, and I notice the eyebrows move with his lips.

"Um, no. I'm just not used to strangers butting into my business. And Miss Havisham! Not even close!" But I think about my disheveled appearance after all the days on the road, the ferry hair, and the bird poop, and I'm certain I could use a little self-care.

Paying as quickly as I can and huffing away, I slide into a twirly chair at a Formica table. I catch a quick glimpse of the Space Needle and the Ferris wheel on the waterfront. Across the aisle, Oliver Twist in a leather jacket sits in a booth next to the windows. He puts his Doc Martens up on the other half of the booth and opens his book. How can he sit there and read with so much to look at?

People seem to plop down in assigned seats, acknowledging

no one else around them. Some have laptops and papers spread out across tables, creating an office that looks like it could suffice for longer than thirty-two minutes. A group of women loaded down with shopping bags sits at a table, drinking white wine out of plastic cups, and toasting to ferry pours, which look rather generous. All while the larger-than-a-tugboat, smaller-than-a-cruise ship hunk of metal gently rocks as it crosses the Sound. Next time, I'm getting a ferry wine.

I take a minute to, A, savor the fact that I just drove across the entire country on my own (take that, Nancy! I have gumption!) and, B, wonder what I'm about to step into. My great-grandpa won this cabin playing poker with some old friends. One guy ended up down and didn't have any money, so he threw in the deed to the dilapidated cabin. My mom and my uncle spent time there as kids, and Uncle Don lived there as an adult. I always imagined coming to visit Greensea when Uncle Don was alive. The forests and the water all made it sound magical, but there never seemed to be the perfect time or enough money to make the big trip. And even though Uncle Don and I were pen pals, we only saw each other a few times. It hurt to see me as I got older and looked more like the sister he remembered and desperately missed.

Across the aisle, the Charles Dickens guy takes a break from his reading. Our eyes meet and my cheeks get warm. My cheeks, and my freckles, have always been a thorn in my side, and they continue to torment me.

I stand up to throw the remains of my snack away, and I'm paralyzed at the garbage cans. There are so many choices—recycling, trash, compostable. I'm not sure if the cup my soup was in is trash or recyclable, and the wooden spoon practically splintered in my mouth, so it's probably not trash. It's too much and might as well be written in French. The contents of each garbage can make the puzzle even more complicated, as it seems every item has been placed in each bin. So I walk down the steps to my car with my garbage in hand and vow to throw it out when I get to the cabin.

The ferry crossing is fast, as promised, and after I throw the trash in the passenger seat, I go to the railing and take several requisite Instagram posts and a dozen selfies with my feet firmly planted on the deck. When I get back to the car, my phone pings with a text from Beth, my BFF and the only reason I hesitated to leave Virginia.

> Beth: Are you almost there? Remember, this doesn't have to be forever. You don't need to stay out there. You can find some island magic and head back east.

> Sylviane: You know I have to see if I can make it work.

I owe it to Uncle Don, and my mom, to at least check it all out and see if I can make Greensea my home. I guess I owe it to myself too. I rub the jade stone in my pocket and feel ready for a new chapter.

So far, the journey's been dreamy.

Before I drive off the ferry, I look back at Tabatha to make sure she's ok. She survived the ten-day trip by living in hotel bathtubs. I wanted as many pieces of home as would fit in Old Blue, so I was determined to take the furry creature with me, along with my mom's old kitty cat cookie jar and my grandma's egg cups. But I've questioned my judgment more than once and wished, several times, I could make the rabbit disappear in her velvet top hat.

"We're almost there, Tabs! We've got this now!"

FOUR

JOSH

Tourists are a menace to society. There's only one boat that leaves the ferry terminal. It goes to one place. You swipe your ticket and walk on the boat. Easy. But somehow people can't figure out how to swipe. Or maybe they've misplaced their ticket between the ticket booth and the twenty yards to the ferry entrance. When they're on the boat, it's like it's their first time being in a public space. They lean over the side. They run and do aerobics. I don't know why people can't just go through the galley, pick their food, and take a seat. It's simple, but people who get on the boat act like they've never seen tater tots before. Or water. The number of times the captain has to announce, "If you came in a car, please exit the boat in your car." Who the hell forgets they've come in a car? Fortunately, the summer is over, and we're back down to mostly residents on the island.

I should have been nicer to the lady who looked a little lost, but my gosh, how many more things was she going to go back for? Decide already. It must've been her first time on the ferry, but she didn't look like a tourist coming over for a day trip. Her chin-length blonde hair was wind-blown, but something about her outfit didn't look like most people coming to check out Greensea. She didn't have a backpack, water bottle, and all the paraphernalia people think they need when they visit. I can't be completely mad that she kept getting out of line since, at least, she had good taste in ferry food.

The ferry makes a wide turn along the shore of Greensea Island. Tiny, older clapboard houses intermix with more modern homes that occupy every inch of the property. Red and yellow kayaks decorate the beach. Tall pine trees rise behind the homes, and mountains peek out in the distance. I don't tire of the view, just the humans.

Every time I get on or off the ferry, my heart rate goes up. Today, I'm driving Dave's truck, which I've filled with a rented cider press, all the bottles for the cider, damn sticks for candied apples, and compostable napkins and silverware. I should leave this all for the heir to take care of, but judging from her emails, that may require me to answer more questions. Who knows what distraction she will come upon before she gets here, anyway? There's so much at the Seattle waterfront. She may go round and round on the Ferris wheel and never get on the ferry. If I can dump all this stuff in the barn, it will be one less thing I have to do later.

The slowpoke from the galley takes selfies at the railing near the cars. Takes a photo, looks at it, then takes another one. She's as decisive with the photos as she was with the food in the checkout line. Regardless of her progress, the boat docks and cars get ready to inch forward. Fantastic! She's in the car in front of me.

"Jesus Christ. These people can't even follow the yellow lines off the boat!"

She's driving her blue Honda like she's never driven before, and all she has to do is follow the car in front of her and stay in her own lane. Instead, she turns her turn signal on, and then off. Brakes. And she's probably about to hit her hazards. Driving off the ferry is just like driving on any other road, or at least, it should be! As soon as we get to the little two-lane part, I zip around the car and lift my hand in Ferry Girl's direction. I'm out of here before she gets confused by the stoplight in front of her. Hopefully, the mysterious island elk won't pop out onto the road, because she'll probably stop traffic and try to take a selfie with it. I don't understand people. I don't care if her hair bounced as she walked. She's a newcomer, and I don't like them.

———

Closing time during fall is my favorite time at Cedar & Fern because it's empty. Locals come early in the day. Everyone settles into their routine at home in the evening. No emergency paddle board rentals or requests for one more pint of our home-made ice cream. I can sit at the cash register and look at the day's sales without being disturbed by anyone other than Sander feeding the chickens before he leaves for the day.

When I hear the door chimes, I yell, "Closing in five minutes," without looking up.

"It won't take that long! Only here for one of your pies to take to the city with me."

I recognize the voice without looking up from the register. Lindsey freaking Dover.

"Oh, hey, Josh! How. Are. You?" asks the strawberry blonde standing in front of me. She might bless my heart next.

"Fine, Lindsey. And you?"

"Good. I mean great. Heading into Seattle to meet Bradley's parents and wanted to bring them a pie straight from the island." Lindsey gives her hair a little flip.

"You're still together?" I ask.

"Yeah." She leans in. "I think he's the one."

"I'm sure he is, Lindsey."

I have so much more to say. Like, of course you fell for the prep school tourist hanging out with his bachelor party buddies at The Old Owl while we were dating. She said dating an islander was casual and almost like inbreeding, so it didn't really count. She had a lot of excuses for why it was okay to cheat on me. But I hold it all in, take a deep breath through my nose, and head to the fridge to get her the pie.

"Thank. You. So. Much, Josh." She annunciates each word as I hand her the pie. "I do hope Quinn isn't still upset about the minor episode with Bradley and his friends at The Old Owl. You know they didn't mean any harm."

The "episode" Lindsey is referring to was their fraternity handshake that got out of control when they were bopping genitals with the server. Quinn barred the guys from The Old Owl and GG had a field day with it.

"Take the pie, Lindsey. It's on us." I already closed out the register, and I'd be happier if she just left. I don't need the extra conversation while she tries to pay me for a pie I'll probably need to mark down tomorrow.

"You sure are the sweetest, Josh Sherman. Thank you."

I nod and lock the door as soon as she leaves.

Reason number 7,001 I want to leave the island: Lindsey Dover and her entourage of frat boys.

FIVE

SYLVIANE

It's five in the evening, and the summer sun is still high in the northern sky. After the ferry ride and a couple of missed turns (I figured it would be easier to get around an island, but I think I've found every dead end there is), I find myself in the middle of downtown. It's like we landed in a different world upon crossing the Sound. I half expect Rory and Lorelai from *Gilmore Girls* to come running across the town square, or Luke's Diner to be perched on the corner. Single-level brick and wood buildings dot the main street. I pass a bookstore called Between the Covers, a toy store, something called Apollo that looks like a coffee shop, and Saltwater Bakeshop. I have an urge to stop and check out each of these little places, but I just want to get to the cabin and see what awaits me.

Way back in Virginia, I grabbed a scrap of paper out of my purse that said, "Forever is composed of nows" (hence all of the stops along the way), and this now is for getting to the cabin.

My phone barks out directions. Turn right here. Proceed

straight for 300 yards. But oh my gosh! There's a peacock on the road. All his feathers are spread eagle. Is that what it's called? Probably not, but that's what it looks like. This is the first peacock I've seen in the wild. He's just strolling across the street without a care in the world. I pull over to the shoulder and grab my cellphone to take a pic, but a biker comes up behind me and blows some kind of air horn.

"Can't stop in a bike lane, lady!" he yells.

Nice impression I'm making on the island already. Jeez, I need to get myself together. The next mile brings llamas and chickens behind wooden fences. Signs advertising local wineries are nailed to trees. I can barely see the outlines of houses obscured behind the gigantic fir trees, but I can feel the magic in the air.

I play "Prius, Prius, Tesla. Prius, Prius, Tesla" as Old Blue hitches down the street. She's the only one of her kind. The electric cars sure don't have the same melody coming from their engine that Old Blue does after the long drive.

I turn down Honeysuckle Lane and realize my cross-country journey is about to end. I've driven three thousand miles away from Nancy and the little world she controlled. I will Old Blue up the hill, turn left, and then down a hill that is making me dizzy, until I find a long gravel drive leading to a log cabin.

A little log cabin with a green roof and a wraparound porch sits tucked behind the trees. The bright red front door and criss-cross windowpanes make it look like a dreamy gingerbread house permanently dressed up for the holidays. It's so cute. It is cuter than anything I could have found on Instagram. It's straight out of a storybook. I put the car in park and sit for a second to take it all in. My new beginning.

I'm slightly worried the grumpy dude didn't really leave the key under the mat for me. But as soon as I lift it up, it's there, and I give it a quick kiss for good luck.

I look around the front porch, take a deep breath, and open the door. My crystals feel heavy in my pocket. I hope the magic I've felt since we got off the ferry continues once I open the door.

Part of me is ready to shriek with joy when I'm hit with the smell of the wood (and must) and see the dark timbers and the light windows (and the cobwebs). It's perfect, sort of. No matter what, it's mine.

The interior walls are logs, just like the exterior. I take a step in, and I'm walking down a hallway, like through a forest, to a wall of windows overlooking a tiny emerald bay. I can clean the cobwebs and buy some candles. The house feels solid. It has good bones. I'll bibbidi-bobbidi-boo the rest of it into shape. I can do this. I will do this. Applehill Farm is mine.

I take my time getting my bearings. Back at the front door, there's an office filled with bookshelves. The kitchen and great room, with the wall of windows, sit at the end of the hallway and are separated by an imposing brick fireplace that reaches to the top of the cathedral ceiling. There's a loft above the great room. An old leather couch sits against a wall of bookcases, opposite the windows. The clay seagull I sculpted in second grade art class sits on a shelf next to a picture of me missing my two front teeth. Dad tried to be good about sending things to Uncle Don when I was young. I smile thinking that he kept these little mementos all these years.

The live-edge wood coffee table holds a pile of dog-eared books, and I imagine Uncle Don spent hours sitting on the couch, feet on the table, book in his lap as he alternated between reading the words in front of him and watching the tide roll in. The layer of dust is cosmetic. I can make the whole place look better.

See-through stairs with fish cut out of the banister stretch from the left of the family room to a lofted space with two bedrooms and a bathroom. The primary bedroom is open and looks down into the great room. Uncle Don's bed is thrown together with an old quilt and quite a few pillows. A pair of slippers sits next to his nightstand, which has towers of books and several mugs filled with stale coffee. It's all ready for him to walk in at any minute.

Next to his room is a small bedroom, with a door, that will be the perfect place for Beth to stay when she visits. There's a twin bed dressed in an old quilt. Both rooms are dated but cozy.

Back downstairs, the kitchen, definitely original to before my uncle, holds the basic appliances. The fridge screams bachelor, with nothing but smelly takeout containers and coffee creamer. And the small pantry has only a box of Grape Nuts and peanut butter. Uncle Don must've been a frequent patron at all the island restaurants.

Sliding glass doors and windows off the kitchen and great room open to the key feature: the bay. The wraparound porch grows even larger on the back side of the house. I make a mental note to find a small table to put out there so I can eat outside until the weather gets too cold—after I clean up all the pine needles and bird poop, of course.

I walk down the steps to the small grassy area at the water's edge, stand on top of the rocks, and look at my reflection in the water. This is it, my house. The first thing I've owned other than Old Blue.

"It's like a snow globe without the snow," I whisper to the fish.

I'm heartbroken that Uncle Don isn't here and I don't have anyone to share all of this with. I kind of feel guilty that I feel hopeful and lucky because of his death.

I send a quick email to J.

Hi!

I'm here. It's perfect! The balcony! The windows! My reflection in the water! I'm living in a fairy tale! I just hope there's not an evil witch ready to walk through the door and pop me into the oven. I can't wait to meet you. Why don't you swing by for coffee? Give me a few days so I can get things together, but we can sit on the deck and watch the birds.

Thank you for keeping everything in tip-top condition.

S.

I lug all of my belongings into the house, feeling oddly relieved that I haven't acquired more. Old Blue's filled to the brim with Tabatha and her cage. I find the perfect home for my rabbit—Uncle Don's office—and tuck the cage next to the oversized lawyer's desk that sits in the center of the room. Why did he need such an official-looking piece of furniture? Seems out of place with the look of the rest of the cabin.

I'm exhausted from the travel and want to curl up in his bed before I begin the daunting task of making this place my own. I check each door several times to ensure they are all locked and make sure the stove I didn't even use is off, just as Dad always reminded me. It's late in Virginia, but I text Beth good night.

Sylviane: Hey! The cabin is lovely! Well, lovely isn't the perfect word. I def need to put some elbow grease into cleaning it up. But I can do it.

Beth: I know you can! You've got this! I'm just a phone call away.

For the first time in quite a while, I think I can do this. I can make a new life for myself right here.

GREENSEA GAZETTE

Hey, hey, Islanders!

The heir has arrived! A hearty island welcome to the newest inhabitant of Applehill Farm, the property built on legends. The old island story was set in motion many decades ago during the yearly poker match between the summer residents and the permanent residents of the island. Big things were on the line during this game of cards. A year's worth of salmon, round-trip ferry tickets, a season of firewood, and, this year in particular, a log cabin. Don Hamilton's family won it free and clear. Let's give a warm reception to Sylviane DuPont, the heir to the lore. We hope you find what you need on this island filled with missed chances, broken hearts, twinkling eyes, loves lost and found, things that are barely standing the test of time, much happiness, and more than a bit of despair.

Sending wishes for a speedy recovery to Mr. Flanagan's eyebrows after an unfortunate accident with a campfire. We're glad there wasn't more damage. Some may say he looks even better without his unibrow! But please remember, until the rains arrive, we still have a burn ban on the island. Save the trees and your face!

We all saw the green Volvo using an expired medical pass to shortcut (emphasis on the cut) the ferry line on the Friday of Labor Day weekend. Darling, you know what they say about Karma.

Small businesses have seen more success this summer, even if Old Man Jackson took his horse and buggy out for a ride, holding up traffic down the entirety of Main Street. By the way, if the horse and buggy can make it around the new roundabout without crossing through the middle, so can your oversized pickup truck.

XOXO,

GG

SIX

SYLVIANE

My first purchase, after oodles of cleaning supplies, will be curtains for the windows. The bedroom faces east, and damn, the sun rises early here. No need to be up at five o'clock every morning.

I want to get my bearings and wander around the house again. I'm like a kid on Halloween inspecting all their candy. This place is all mine, and I want to memorize it and fall in love with it.

I didn't know Uncle Don well enough to know his habits or what his daily routine looked like, and it feels strange to jump into his life, or at least, his house. The dishwasher still has his dishes in it. Fiestaware plates sit in piles in the single cabinet next to the almost-empty refrigerator. His clothes are still in the dryer. Do I put them in a bag for Goodwill? Do I save them? What do I do with the mismatched socks he'll never wear again?

The pages in his books are dog-eared, waiting for his return. I hadn't thought about his stuff. I kept imagining coming here to a fully furnished house minus an occupant. I never thought about having to get rid of the things he used every day. The house oozes Uncle Don's energy, and until I learn all there is to know about him, I don't want to change too much. I'm mourning the things I never told him, the time we didn't spend together, and the loss of a human I knew. But I'm also struck by this gift that he gave me.

My stomach growls, and I'm not in the mood for the stale Grape Nuts in the pantry, so I walk back upstairs to get dressed. I open my duffel for the umpteenth time and vow to find a place to put my things until I find a home for Uncle Don's things.

The temperature in the car says 58 degrees—definitely not as warm as it is in Virginia at this time of year. People wearing flannels and shorts walk up and down Main Street. My entire wardrobe is going to need an overhaul in this place, because I don't look the PNW part yet—not to mention I'm probably not prepared for the weather. Pack away the tank tops and the sandals. This place feels like you need solid clothing and footwear. The bright floral sundress I threw on is not the vibe I should have opted for if I wanted to fit in.

I find a parking spot and smell my way to the bakery. As soon as I open the door, I'm blasted with the smell of cinnamon and sugar. It's warm and cozy, and the goose bumps on my arms are going away, so I never want to leave. Banjo music plays in the background. Frosted sugar cookies shaped like beach balls, whales, and backpacks fill glass cases, along with danishes, croissants, and cakes frosted with every type of decoration. My stomach decides it wants one of everything. I look at the menu and notice a piece of toast for $7.00.

"What's your toast served with?" I ask the brunette behind the counter.

"A side of butter."

"And it's $7.00?"

"Yes, ma'am. We make our bread with locally sourced wheat

and bake it in open air ovens that sit along the Salish Sea, flavoring the bread with our unique sea air. We hand cut every slice of toast."

I never thought slicing bread by hand was a selling point. At least, it isn't one I've ever heard before. Part of me wants to order the overpriced, pompous piece of bread just to see what's so special, and part of me wants to find a McDonald's to grab an Egg McMuffin, but I'm here, and I remember I'm on an island and there probably isn't a fast-food chain, anyway.

"What would you like?" asks the person behind the counter.

"What's in the hummingbird cake?"

"Hummingbird cake is a dense cake made with spices and locally grown and dried organic fruits," recalls the girl, as if she's memorized a script.

"Do you have anything plain, like a croissant or maybe a blueberry muffin?"

"We have a vegan blueberry scone made with blueberries from one of the original pieces of acreage on the island, farmed by Japanese farmers after they returned from internment, and a croissant au beurre made with butter from the milk of cows that...."

A book slams closed behind me.

"For Pete's sake! Will you just pick something from the glass counter you've been standing in front of for the last ten minutes?"

I dig my nails into my palms and turn around to find "Oliver," dressed again in the same leather jacket and black Doc Martens. Ferry Guy is back.

"Jeezus. You're like one of those electric cars. You just sneak up on people out of nowhere." I'm conscious of how close we are, and I hope I used a satisfactory amount of toothpaste. "And what is it you recommend?"

He looks at me, mouth askew like he's attempting not to

smile. "For dessert, I like the chocolate vegan applesauce cake. For breakfast, you can't go wrong with the toast, even though they should roll it in gold flakes at that price. But the humming-bird cake is never to be missed."

I roll my eyes, but what is it about that sideways mouth that stirs something inside of me?

"One piece of cake, a piece of toast, and a nonfat iced hazelnut latte, please." I'll save the other treats for a rainy morning that needs some warmth. I take Dad's American Express card out of my wallet and hand it to the cashier. He insisted I keep his credit card, which I've had for years, until I'm settled and in case there were an emergency on the road.

"I'm out of your way, Oliver." I eye his book. Dickens again. "Do you only carry hardcover books around so you can get the attention of unsuspecting strangers?"

"Best way to read the classics," he answers.

"Making your way through Dickens?"

"It's back-to-school time. Who doesn't take a moment to read a story of redemption and rebirth?"

"I guess it's always the best of times and the worst of times." I smirk.

"Hmmm..." His eyes smolder with a hint of something he might want to say behind all that get-out-of-my-way.

I've always dreamed about finding someone to discuss litera-ture with everywhere, even in a checkout line. My idea of pillow talk is arguing the merits of *Mrs. Dalloway*. Thinking of this guy's moody dark eyebrows hitting my pillow makes me blush. One corner of his mouth turns up as he...Stop! Who has thoughts like these in the middle of a bakery? I blink rapidly to get rid of the thought of him in my bed.

I retreat quickly and grab my food from the counter.

"See ya, Ferry Guy."

"See ya, Ferry Girl," replies the stranger.

My phone pings with a message from Nancy.

> Nancy: $34.00 at "Saltwater Bakeshop." Bit
> excessive, even for you. Are you feeding an
> army?

Shit. I forgot that even though we're in different time zones, Nancy would still get notifications about my expenditures right away. I never take advantage of the card, and breakfast should fall within the well-defined limits. Dad gave me the card when I was in college, after I came home on the train for Thanksgiving break and didn't have money for a taxi to the house. I couldn't get ahold of Dad to pay the cab fare, and no one was home. I walked next door to Mrs. Montuori's house and borrowed money from her. It was the height of embarrassment for Nancy, and since she couldn't tell me not to come home, she made Dad give me a card to be used in emergency situations—also known as situations that may embarrass her and not necessarily things that threaten my life. Years went by with me having the card, and Dad had me keep it, "just in case." He couldn't give me much security growing up, so this was something that made him feel better about his shortcomings.

> Sylviane: Just me. A little end of my journey
> celebration! Thank you!

I stroll down the street and find a bench to sit on and eat my breakfast. Every store window still has a summer display. There's a pyramid of stuffed animals with sunglasses and backpacks in the toy store. A mountain made of CBD gummies in the health food store. An umbrella with ferries dangling from each spoke in some sort of gift shop.

I look down Main Street. It's like a little town you'd visit on vacation, but people live here. I pinch myself. It's a dream come true.

I've put my suburban-sprawl life to bed and come to an idyllic little island. Most of the stores are still closed, but it looks like people are walking in and out of the bookstore with newspapers, so I decide to walk in. I need a book anyway, because I'm sure Uncle Don doesn't have any romances on his bookshelf to keep me warm at night.

The wood floor creaks and announces my presence in the store. I walk around and find a used book section where I'm certain Ferry Guy must shop. It takes a minute, but I find the romance section, which I figured would be substantial in a store named Between the Covers. I find two and walk to the counter.

"Oh, you will love these!" the college-aged girl at the register proclaims.

"Thanks!" I hand her my emergency credit card. I'm not in the mood for small talk.

"Hmmm...Your card is being denied. Do you have another one? Maybe it didn't transfer with the move." The bookseller hands the black card back to me.

Move? How'd she know I moved? Word travels fast in this town, I guess. But even more strange is that Dad's card doesn't work.

Touché...Nancy must have canceled it. I suck in a scream bubbling in my throat and hand the cashier my card so I can get out of the bookstore. My cheeks feel flushed, and I'm dying from embarrassment. I fiddle in my bag for my crystals to get some sense of calm.

A simple breakfast was enough for her to cut me off? How can I possibly be a threat to her when I'm on an island in the middle of nowhere? I could call my dad, but it would leave him feeling worse about everything. He'd fumble for the right words when I told him. Just like he did when Nancy convinced him parents didn't go to dance recitals or fifth grade graduations. He doesn't know how to do anything but agree with her and shake his head. He's powerless where she's concerned, and I wonder if he was really like that with my mom, or if losing her and being left with a daughter to raise on his own left him feeling so desperate that he was easy prey for Nancy. I won't win any confrontation with Nancy. I'll only end up feeling worse, and I don't need to be an almost-thirty-year-old throwing a tantrum in the middle of my new town. The power struggle between Nancy and me needs to end, and living out here, thousands of miles away, is for the best.

Before I go home, I stop at the grocery store to pick up something to fill the pantry and get some vinegar to clean the cabin. The grocery store's like a bigger version of the cafeteria on the ferry. Aisles of organic treats I can't afford. Local farm-grown veggies and fruit. It's beautiful and peaceful. I pick up a few treats for myself anyway, and then grab some frozen pizzas, paper towels, and cinnamon. I'll sprinkle it into the wash, my dish soap, even my shampoo. Cinnamon hides all the unpleasant odors, even old log cabin smells.

As I'm walking up to the counter, I stop. Uncle Don died in a grocery store. Am I in the exact place where he died? My feet won't let me take another step.

"Ma'am? Can I help you?" asks a teenaged boy standing at the end of the self checkout.

"Ummm...Well, is this the only grocery store on the island?"

"Sure is! Island Grocers started about seventy-five years ago and is proud to still be the only grocery store on the island. There are other markets, like Cedar & Fern and Sully's. Oh, and the gas station has a few things, but we are the only place you can find everything you need."

He's smiling, clearly proud of his position at the store. But I feel like I should kneel and recite a prayer. This, this store, is where my uncle, the only living relative of my dead mother, died.

"Are you checking out or just thinking?" asks a voice behind me. I turn to find a woman clad in an all-white workout outfit. She's perfect, like she just stepped out of an Instagram ad for a workout video and didn't actually sweat. Every hair shellacked to her head and held by a tight bun. Her makeup has one of those natural looks that probably took tons of products to achieve. Dressed like an angel but giving devil energy.

"Sorry. Just thinking." Instead of saying a prayer, I pay for my groceries using my credit card and hope the dwindling bank account will make if for another few days, until I can find a job as a reporter or a magic gig.

I load the groceries into Old Blue and look up at the sky before I start her.

"Thank you, Uncle Don. Thank you for this gift."

No one's given me anything before. Well, that's not totally true. I got a few birthday and Christmas gifts because Nancy couldn't shop for Caroline and get nothing for me. But while Caroline got the latest and greatest, I got things from the previous season's clearance rack. But not now...My luck has changed.

SEVEN

JOSH

Living above the store allows me to go back and forth from work whenever I want. I can run down for a delivery and come back up when I need to switch gears. My place is small. It's like the store has to be my extended living space, otherwise my studio apartment would feel like an oversized dorm room. Don't get me wrong, it has its benefits. Vaulted ceilings. A view of the Sound. Old, solid hardwood floors. I updated the kitchen and the bathroom with modern appliances and stainless steel fixtures. And it hardly costs me a penny compared to other places on this island.

I keep thinking about my run-in with Ferry Girl at the bakery. I might go earlier tomorrow in order to spare myself an extra ten minutes of her indecisiveness. Or I'll go at the same time and see if she's still wearing clothes that seem woefully inappropriate for the weather. As soon as the rains and the Big Dark arrive, she'll have to shed the little strappy dresses and flip-flops. She's quick with the literature quips though, and it adds a little something different to my routine of bakery, hike, work, but the tradeoff of time wasted may not be worth it.

As I sit at my kitchen table, an old slab of maple they used at the bakery to knead their dough, doubling as my office and my eating space, my level of annoyance increases when I get an email.

Dear J.,

This entire island is magical. The town square, the gazebo, the quaint shops! It's out of this world. And I feel like I'm a full-fledged islander already. Somehow, everyone knows my name. What's your favorite place to eat here? I read about Codmother's. Could that name be any cuter?

S.

Greensea's her new start and my interminable prison. She won't have to buy any sugar while she lives at Applehill Farm, since her syrupy attitude just oozes out of her. Get a grip, lady. This island is not all sugar and spice and everything nice. There are lots of reasons it's more snips and snails. One: tourists. Two: rain. Three: it gets dark. Four: old girlfriends. Five: people who don't know how to drive at an appropriate speed. Meeting her will be like pulling a piece of duct tape off my hairy leg. I'll do it, but not yet.

Out of familial obligation, I can only recommend one spot.

The Old Owl
J.

A waft of sourdough comes through my window. Norma must've made her delivery. I have a hard time not bolting down to grab a warm loaf only the ping of my email stops me.

J.,

Oh yes! I have to try it. I'd love to meet you and thank you in person for all you've done for me and Applehill Farm. Let me know when you're free to stop over.
Thanks again!

S.

No way I'm going to send a response to the heir right away. I don't need a pen pal. Before I know it, I'll be trading scratch 'n sniff stickers and making paper fortune tellers. Slice of sourdough, then a response.

Norma's been making our bread for longer than I've been alive. Her loaves are light and airy with the perfect tang. Legend has it, her starter's the sibling of a hundred-year-old starter from San Francisco. Our freshly churned butter practically melts across the slice. Things like this make my studio apartment more than bearable.

Soon.
J.

Ping. Does she live in front of her laptop?

J.,

I hope I haven't done anything to offend you. I'm super grateful you took care of this property. I imagine you were close to my uncle, and I'm sorry for your loss. I didn't know him as well as I would've liked. Since you were friends, maybe you can tell me more about him. Dinner at my place this Saturday at 5:30? I can cook for any dietary restrictions you may have.

S.

Any dietary restrictions? Blue plate special time? Does she think I'm one of Don's old cronies? Screw it. I don't care who she thinks I am. A momentary handoff of information, and then I can focus on my new horizons.

I click over to my resumé to make sure it's up to date. Not going to leave this place without keeping it current. My objective is easy: cartographer seeking a position to apply mapping techniques to worthwhile projects. And I'll determine the worthiness of the project by what's going on on Greensea if I ever get offered a job.

There are few positions anywhere in the United States for someone with my skill set. I wish some brave career counselor had mentioned that when I was in college. People look at me like I've received an advanced degree in calligraphy. Instead, I'm sidled with a degree that means I'm better at being a manager of retail establishments, something I'm not that keen on, than what I studied for four years. I get the occasional exciting project, but those are few and far between. If an opportunity comes around, I need to take it. It's the only way forward for me.

In college, geology and the study of the earth thrilled me. And then I longed to map the topography of the Puget Sound. I get it, there are very few nineteen-year-olds interested in anything like that. But Mom and Dad pushed us to study what interested us. Dave studied biology with a concentration in marine life and ended up an oyster farmer. Oliver and Jac chose more practical and mainstream careers, accountant and teacher respectively. Some days I think Dad encouraged me to pursue mapmaking so he'd have someone to take over the store, because there'd be no way I'd get another job.

I'll stop by soon. No dinner necessary.
J.

EIGHT

SYLVIANE

I don't understand why J is so grumpy. I guess what they say about not knowing what's going on in other people's lives is true, it's hard to imagine anything based on the few words we've exchanged.

I check my phone before I put the keys in the ignition and see that Ryder texted.

> Ryder: I'm in town. I'll come over tonight.

Ha! I'm about to give him a shock.

> Sylviane: I moved, Ryder.

> Ryder: Great. Give me the new address and I'll come over.

> Sylviane: Like across the country.

My phone rings.

"Trix!" He uses the nickname he gave me when I took my first magic class. He knows it will cut right to my heart. "What the hell is going on?"

I tell him the abbreviated story of inheriting the cabin.

"Why didn't you tell me? I would have helped you move!"

The actual answer is that I want to limit the number of times I have to watch him walk away. Ryder always walks away, and I need to be strong and turn the page on that life. Oh, yeah, and he's engaged.

"It's all good, Ryder. I know you're busy."

"If you need anything, let me know. And I'll figure out a way to get out there soon."

Of course he would. Having the money he does lets him go all over the world without a care.

The first time I went out with Ryder, he was all glitter and glitz. He told me he'd be at my apartment the next day at eleven, a daytime date. He left no room for a no. At 10:05, a brown box arrived, filled with an evening gown in the palest blue. At 10:59, he knocked on the door. A refurbished VW bus, filled with some of his friends dressed in their finery, sat at the curb. We drove an hour into the hills to a zipline course I was certain was closed to the public. He attached me to my harness and, one by one, we sailed through the trees in evening wear. I'd never ziplined before, and my stomach was in my mouth, and my fingers burned from the death grip I used to hold on to the straps. But his soft hazel eyes led the way and calmed my butterflies. We landed in an orchard filled with food carts; a Food Cart Rodeo, he called it. Sampling street tacos and beignets drizzled in caramel sauce. Racing from cart to cart dressed in fancy clothes. Laughing with friends who apparently went to grad school with us, but I hadn't met any of them while I worked in the cafeteria or studied in the library. The day into the night was carefree, easy, and the most over-the-top thing I'd ever done.

I was used to checking prices and carefully determining the merits of any action. On that adventure, no one worried about money once. But none of that was what drew me to him. It was the way he touched my arm and looked into my eyes when he told me the most inane facts about carne asada. I felt like I was cuddled up under a weighted blanket when he was talking to me. I'd always wanted that kind of love, and I thought I'd finally found it. And as quickly as he came into my life that day in grad school, he boomeranged in and out of it. I should've followed Maya Angelou's sage advice, "When someone shows you who they are, believe them." Because I knew Ryder would never be with me permanently, and if he came to Greensea, I knew he would also leave Greensea.

To make matters worse, the only thing I could have done to curry Nancy's favor was to make Ryder fall in love with me. Like actually ask me to marry him. Nancy's eyes lit up when she talked about him. Unfortunately, Dick and Sloane Rockenbok, Ryder's parents, were not interested in his marrying the nonpedigreed, sort-of orphan from the side of the tracks where they only had white picket fences instead of gated driveways.

But none of that stopped Ryder from popping in and wooing me every so often. Making me believe I was the only girl in the world. Taking me to dinner. Listening intently. Asking all the right questions. And then leaving before the sun rose. That can't happen again. Time for me to take care of my heart.

———

I tie my hair back with a bandana and wish I'd gotten it cut before I left Virginia. My cleaning uniform is a pair of overalls and a tank top. Look the part, be the part.

But where to start? I need to unpack my own stuff, so I'll start with Don's clothes. I walk into his closet. Not spending enough time with Uncle Don means I don't recognize any of his clothing. The few times I saw him, when he brought my grandparents to visit, I was still in elementary school. But they both died before I went to middle school.

There are about a dozen shirts of varying shades of blue, a couple of pairs of jeans, some khakis, and a super dusty suit. There's a tan canvas sunhat on a hook in the back. Some dirty work boots and a pair of muddy hiking boots. T-shirts, socks, and underwear fill the dresser. I feel a little like a Peeping Tom going through his drawers, and I don't want to touch his underwear, but I keep them folded and place them in bags. He didn't have a lot of clothes, so it doesn't take long to pack them away and carry them down to the office. I hang my own things up slowly, honoring the changing of the guard.

———

After a day of scrubbing to make this place shine like the top of the Chrysler building, I can't wait to get in the tub. Soak all this dirt off of me. I take my sage out of my suitcase and burn some to clear the energy out of the cabin, my cabin, while the water's running in the tub.

As I grab one of Uncle Don's towels, I feel a breeze above my head, like something's swooping by. I run my hand through my hair and something grazes it. Whatever it is is flying. Did a bird get in the house? I look around and see two little beady eyes glowing in the corner of the room, just as another flying thing dive-bombs my nose. They're bats. Freaking bats! Flying around the room.

I flick on the light and run into the bathroom, shutting the door. I breathe for a second and wonder if I'll have to spend the rest of the night here. Doing a quick scan of the ceiling, I don't see any flying rodents, but my feet are wet. There's a shallow pool of brown water on the floor. The tub must've run over while the bats distracted me. But brown? What the hell?

Holy shit! It's like a rust bomb is coming out of the faucet. The whole tub is filled with sequoia-colored water. I turn the water off and try the sink. Brown as well.

Okay. I can't leave the bathroom, because there are bats outside the door. Step one: wipe up the water from the floor. Step two: wrap a towel on my head so the bats can't nest in my hair. Step three: run around to each room, turning on lights. There. Those mofos will stay away now.

But what do I do about the water? Step four: become a plumber. No landlord, or Dad, to call for help. Whenever we had a water issue at home, Dad tinkered with the kitchen sink. It has to hold the answers to my problem now.

The faucet in the kitchen is running brown too. But the large pipe under the sink doesn't hold any clues. There aren't any magic buttons or levers. What was I expecting? A fuse box for water issues?

The brown water is harder to figure out. What kind of water system does this island have? Is water from the bay coming up into the house?

Somehow, I've got this. I have no choice. With all the lights on, the bats will stay away. I google bats and log cabins and learn quickly that log cabins are one of their favorite hangouts, and once they mark a house, they keep coming back for years and years. The little crevices that exist around all the logs are perfect places for the bats to hide out. Great. Just what I wanted to hear. Maybe my new trope is Snow White, and I'm one with the forest animals. Then where are all my dwarves ready to help me out?

The front closet must have something I can use to catch a bat if it comes near me, but all I can find are a couple of pickle-ball paddles that will have to do.

Emailing Mr. Grumpy Pants doesn't seem like the best idea, because he'll only answer with one word, and it probably won't be a helpful one.

There were papers somewhere in the kitchen. Maybe there's a "what to do if" list or something. But I doubt it, because why would a grown man who lives alone need to leave himself a list of what to do?

The fridge has a couple of phone numbers. Dave. Maya. Shea. But not much else. I can call the numbers or figure out a solution. My degree is journalism and not plumbing. I look at the numbers on the fridge again and decide to dial Dave. It can't hurt. What's the worst that can happen? They hang up on me?

After five rings a guy answers. "Hello?"

"Hi, is this Dave?" I ask.

"Yes," he drawls.

"This is Sylviane DuPont. I saw your phone number on my uncle's refrigerator."

"Okay." Slowly again. "Who's your uncle?"

"Don. Don Hamilton."

"Ahhh. Okay. Are you at the cabin?" he asks.

"Yes. Got here last night, and tonight I noticed all the water's brown, and there's a bat or two swarming around my head."

Dave lets out a laugh.

"It's not funny!" If these things are laughable to islanders, I better take a crash course on becoming a handyman or exterminator while I develop a harder exterior and a love for rustic living.

"You're right. I'm sorry. It's just funny that you're getting indoctrinated into island life so quickly."

"Well, if this is island life, I'm not sure I'm cut out for it."

It's not fair to ask this guy to come over tonight, so I need to figure out a plan to make it until he can come over.

"Any chance you can stop by tomorrow?"

"Um. Yeah. I can come by in the morning."

"Thanks."

I'll sleep with the lights on and keep my head under the covers and paddles next to me just in case I need them. I can live without water. In fact, I bet there's a bottle in Old Blue.

Better luck is starting tomorrow. I can feel it.

GREENSEA GAZETTE

Islanders,

Is the newest Islander amongst us already having money issues? A little mouse told me her credit card was declined at Between the Covers, and she may or may not have been adding up her purchases at Island Grocers. How bad can it be when she got a free house?!

Speaking of Island Grocers, we've noticed there's a gum wall starting on Greensea behind the grocery store. Kudos to the "artist" who's created a portrait of Mayor Nickerbottom all out of gum, but let's leave that landmark for Seattle and keep it off our precious island. It's hard to imagine what Keep Greensea Green would have to say about gum. We may not want to broach the topic in case gum goes the way of balloons. With all the coffee this island consumes, gum is a necessary evil.

There's a new donut on the island at Saltwater Bakeshop, but maybe it should take the next boat to somewhere else. Who has ever heard of a honey glazed donut stuffed with real crab? Have you tried it? We toed the line with a garnish of bacon, but we draw the line with seafood.

XOXO,

GG

NINE

SYLVIANE

The sun rises early again and catches me off guard. Little ripples of bright pink and orange clouds make the sky look like it's on fire. The hues shift like an artist mixing colors on their palette. It's so peaceful. The color of the sky mellows to a pale blue, and the green water ripples in the breeze. Evergreens dip down just above the water's edge. An enormous bird with a white beak and tail soars down and perches in a tree across the bay. I squint and try to get a better look. A bald eagle? It can't be. Those things are rare. No way I'd be lucky enough to see one so quickly. Or maybe this is the start of my new luck. At least the sun's up, and I only have to worry about the flying things on the other side of the window.

The cabin has a little chill this morning. I grab some cutoffs out of the dresser and throw on my flip-flops, and grab one of Uncle Don's flannels and throw it over my tank top. With no water, I need to get some coffee. There was some sort of garden shed on the main road with a sign that said coffee. Might as well try that.

Old Blue sputters to life, probably asking what I'm doing up so early, and I attempt to remember where I saw the shed. My memory takes me back toward the grocery store, and I find a few more streets to turn down. Eventually, I find the shed, and it's cuter than I remembered and doesn't resemble a shed. It looks like a hobbit house, with a rounded brown door made out of slabs, a green sloped roof, and a water wheel on one side. A window next to the front door acts as a drive-up window.

"Can I help you?" a teenaged girl asks at the window.

The chalkboard menu has all the standard choices and a bunch of local ones. Pickles Harbor Pistachio Macchiato. Foggy Grays Bay Latte. Greensea Goat Chai. The choices overwhelm me.

"A medium nonfat vanilla latte, please."

Save the adventure for another day. I never expected a drive-thru coffee place on the island, but I'm pleasantly surprised by this quaint little one. The barista hands me my latte with a yawn and thrusts a credit card reader my way.

When I get home, there's a cute little vintage red pickup truck, like the ones you see in Christmas movies, sitting in the driveway. Hmm. There's no one in the orchard. If the person was coming to the barn, they'd probably park closer to it. I open the door to the cabin, peeking in slowly. Ax murderers rarely have vehicles that are recognizable. Binging Netflix has taught me they like to stay under the radar.

"Hello?" No one answers. "Hey, it's Sylviane," I call out as I tiptoe into the family room, ready to turn around and run at any moment.

There's a ladder with a pair of jeans reaching up into the ceiling. Phew. Okay. Must be that Dave guy.

"Hi! I'm so glad you're here. I hate birds. I know bats aren't birds, they're rodents, but they look like birds, and I'm worried that the bats are carrying rabies, and who knows where else they're hiding in here. They could be anywhere."

No reply.

I see a plaid shirt now. The guy turns around, screams, drops his flashlight, and grabs onto the logs to steady himself so he doesn't fall off the ladder, then pulls out his earbuds.

Shit. I scared him. Not the other way around.

"I'm sorry! I said hi right away so you would know I was here, and I wouldn't frighten you. I didn't realize you had earbuds in."

"Yeah, had my music playing loud enough that I never heard you," he explains, climbing down the ladder. He steps onto the ground and still towers over me.

"Dave Sherman." He reaches out a hand.

"Sylviane, Don's niece."

He's tall. Looks like a lumberjack. Plaid shirt. Maybe you're required to put one on as you cross over on the ferry. Dark hair that's kind of floppy, for lack of any other word.

"Thanks for coming over. How'd you get in?" I'm certain I locked the door on my way out.

"Key's hidden in a little box in the third apple tree on the left." He shrugs.

Yikes. Anyone could've walked in over the last two days. How much do other people know about this house, my house? And I know so little about everything, including Uncle Don. A little breeze runs through the cabin and I remember I don't have a bra on, and I'm looking rather pert. I wrap the flannel around myself and Dave pretends he's looking at something else.

"I ran the water through. It looks okay. Sometimes it just looks brown like that. You're at the end of the city water line out here. Seems like I've heard people complain about its color every once in a while. Just let it run for a bit, and you should be fine."

Brown water problem solved. Pretty much just live with it.

"I don't see any obvious ways for the bats to come in. Let's just imagine you had the door open for too long or something and one flew in. They only need a tiny space to come through."

I had the door propped open for a bit yesterday to smell the sea air. It's my new favorite scent, especially when it's mixed with pine.

"You're probably right," I answer. Hopefully this non-answer will make me feel better enough to sleep at three A.M. Add screen door to the list of things I must buy for the cabin.

"Oh, and I put that rabbit back in its cage."

Shit. I forgot I let Tabatha out before I left. "Thank you so much! I use her in my magic tricks."

He shakes his head. "I don't want to know."

I set my coffee down on the table. "Thanks for coming over."

"Anytime. Might be a little later in the day next time, if it's not an emergency." Dave winks as he walks toward the door.

My cheeks blush and I smile. "Thanks."

"This piece of property has its fair share of quirks. Don was a live-off-the-land guy. Hope it's not too rustic for you."

"No, definitely not too rustic for me." Although I do hate camping...But since the cabin has indoor plumbing, it's a marked step up. "I rented in Virginia. This is the first thing I've ever owned."

Dave whistles.

"Pretty nice starter home, if you ask me."

I look around and know the eagle was a sign this morning. He's right. My luck has changed. I've got this!

TEN

JOSH

The beers are flowing at The Old Owl for trivia night. Quinn, our cousin, begged me to come. Probably more like Jac called Quinn and told her I needed to do something other than work, and then Quinn pretended to need me here. Anyway, I'm here, and so is Dave.

Quinn took over The Old Owl from my grandpa. I'm supposed to like it here because it's a family heirloom, but I actually do like it here, even without its relationship to our fam.

The building sits at the base of Grays Bay. There is plenty of deck seating with fire pits at each table. Windows offer sweeping views of the bay. Shiplap walls decorate the inside. Fishing nets drape across the ceiling, and buoys from crab pots hang on the walls. Of course, since it is The Old Owl, a large stuffed owl watches over the bar. Legend has it this owl lived in the tree outside the bar for many years, calling to my grandfather every night as he walked to his truck. One day my grandpa found him lying in the bed of his truck, dead from natural causes, like he was asking to be saved for posterity.

Dave and I are sitting inside at one of the tall tables near the bar.

"Took care of the bats and the brown water at the cabin," he says.

"Oh, for the new person?" I ask. Shit. I should have known that, since I'm taking care of the place. I dropped everything off at the barn but didn't see anyone around.

"Yeah, she found my number on Don's fridge. Water was running brown, and she saw a bat." Dave takes a sip of beer.

"Surprised she didn't email me a novella about it."

"Email you?" Dave asks.

"Yeah. I've been exchanging emails with her ever since Shea, Don's lawyer, gave me her info."

I'll add getting over to the cabin to the to-do list for tomorrow after my hike.

"Surprised you didn't get over there faster. She's cute." Dave smiles.

"Cute?" Her emails seem more annoying than cute. "You going to find more things to fix for her?"

"Nah. Well. Maybe."

"Too married to your oysters?" Dave's an oyster farmer, and those saltwater creatures monopolize a lot of his time. "Thinking of showing her your oyster farm?" I ask, taking a sip of my beer.

"Don't make it sound gross, weirdo."

Dave and his oysters. I have to give him credit, because he's seized on the popularity of the Billion Oyster Project in New York and turned it into an entrepreneurial venture here on Greensea. Dave is happy here and I can't imagine him anywhere else. He's the definition of old Greensea. Goes with the flow and the tide. No rush to get anywhere. Content with what he has, whereas I can't wait to escape and think about myself and my trajectory.

"What'd she look like?" I ask.

"About this tall." He holds up his hand to shoulder height. "Blonde hair all the same length."

Hmm. Wait a second. It can't be. Can it? Could it be the person I keep seeing? The indecisive one on the ferry, and then at Saltwater?

"Where's she from?"

"I didn't get all that. I got the impression she might be from somewhere warm, with her tiny tank top and flip-flops."

It must be Ferry Girl. Maybe she's less annoying in person.

"Didn't seem like an after Labor Day outfit, if you ask me."

Labor Day marks fall for us. Greensea islanders don't just put away the white; we get all the flannel out. Sometimes we're known to wear a knit hat too. We're slowly settling in for the Big Dark.

"I'll head over there tomorrow and check things out. I ran to the city the other day to buy some things for Harvest Fest," I remind him.

Dave laughs.

"What?" I ask.

"She didn't strike me as someone who would be much help with Harvest Fest. She's never even owned a piece of property."

Figures. Not like I thought Don's relative would be a closet festival organizer, but I hoped they would at least know their way around an orchard and a barn. Or have amazing organizational skills. Jury's still out on that, I suppose. I'll have to go see for myself.

"Don't you have some extra time to help me with the store or Applehill Farm? Can't you leave your precious shellfish for a bit?"

"Hmm...Well now that I've seen the new occupant, I may be interested in helping."

Why does Dave need an ulterior motive to help, and I do

things just because? Definitely seems like it's a problem with me and not him, but it still irks me.

I check my messages when I get home. No surprise, there's a message from her.

J.,

Did Don ever mention the bats at Applehill Farm? A couple flew by my head last night. I called this guy Dave, and he came over and didn't see any way for them to get in. But I'm not convinced they can't, so I'm sleeping with the lights on. And under the covers. Just in case. Even with the bats, I still love it here. I spent the afternoon checking out the trees. Looks like there are four types of apple trees out there. I'll have to ask an expert (is there one on the island?) but I think there are Honey Crisp, Gala, Red Delicious, and Granny Smith. I only picked apples once in college with my roommate's family. My stepmother always thought it was too much work to take us out to the mountains and to an orchard, so I never experienced a day in an orchard with all those doughnuts and things made from apples. I wince every time I see a friend's family photo amongst a bunch of apple trees. It's a reminder of the things I missed out on as a kid. I guess it's my turn to change that narrative now! Talk soon.

S.

The least I can do is ask a polite question. Nothing better to do as I sit in bed.

Never heard about any bats. Which mountains?
J.

I put the laptop on top of the pile of books I use as a nightstand. Assuming it's her, Ferry Girl, I might try to be a little nice.

J.,

The Blue Ridge! They're rolling hills compared to the mountains out here. Oh, and the way the mountains changed from east to west is fascinating. They're so jagged out here and velvety in the east. And nothing in the middle. I could see all the way through Illinois to Wisconsin.

Is it weird that I feel so much more connected to the land here? I know it's only been a few days, but instead of passing strip mall after strip mall, I see evergreens, birds, and mountains. Things feel more primal, if you will. I watch the tides from the couch and wake with the sun. I'm in tune with something I never noticed before.

S.

I picture Ferry Girl taking her time, looking at all her surroundings. Getting off at an exit and being overwhelmed by the choices provided by the roadside fast-food signs. She's right though, we are in touch with nature here.

Water (and island living) has a habit of forcing you to pay more attention to your surroundings. Look up friluftsliv.
J.

It will take her a minute to look that up.

J.,

Whoa! I pride myself on being "wordy," if you will, but I've never heard that word before! Friluftsliv—life in the fresh air. What a beautiful word for what I'm feeling! On a serious note, like do I need flood insurance? Or an evacuation plan if there's a tidal wave? These are the things that are going to keep me up tonight while I'm hiding from the bats.

S.

Get out the friendship bracelet string. I've got a new BFF.

Have you ever met a stranger?
J.

J.,

I'm not sure what you mean, but I'm great at talking to people. I love hearing their stories. Like I wonder what the teenaged barista's story is at the hobbit coffee spot.

S.

My smile is threatening my persona.

The barista doesn't have a story, other than her parents are forcing her to work there.
J.

ELEVEN

JOSH

Grand Greensea Forest is the only place where I can think. Miles of trails lined by fir trees circle around the highest point on the island. I know the trails better than the lines on my palm and can walk for a fair amount of time seeing no one else. No matter what the temperature is, it's always cooler in the forest thanks to the marine layer. I love mornings at this time of year. I can feel fall in the air, hear it in the breeze, and see it in the light.

A scream distracts me from my solitude. I walk up a slight hill and see someone on the ground below me.

"GD owl!" I recognize this voice from somewhere and see Ferry Girl's blonde hair poking out of the leaves as she lies in a heap on the trail.

"Well, well, well. What do we have here?" I ask, deciding I'll wait until she's in a less compromising position to tell her she's been emailing me.

"You've got to be kidding me! How many people live on this

island? I've been here for three days, and I keep running into *you*?"

"From the looks of the position you're in, I'd say you're pretty lucky I just ran into you." I take a few steps closer.

"That owl swooped down right above my head. It was going to attack me!" She pulls some leaves from her hair.

"Barn owls. They're all over in here. They like ponytails." I point to the little one on top of her head. "Just annoying, won't do too much damage."

"I have a thing for birds with claws." Ferry Girl groans, and I reach down and offer her a hand up. This close, I can see a small constellation of freckles across the bridge of her nose.

"I can do it on my own." And she pushes herself up to standing.

I bend down to pick up the scraps of paper that are scattered around as if a fortune cookie factory exploded.

"Oh, sorry." She reaches frantically for as many as she can, grabs and stuffs them into her bag.

I read one. "'Forever is composed of nows.' Dickinson. You a fan?"

Her cheeks get red. "Who isn't?"

Good point. "Are these quotes?" I ask, handing her some more.

"Yep. I write things I want to remember on scraps of paper. I stick them in my bag or my pockets. Really anywhere, and everywhere. They must've fallen out when I fell. Sorry. Thank you. I'm a mess."

My favorite things, other than maps, are words. I collect them like my brothers collect cardboard coasters from breweries. I reread the classics and get something new from them every time, and from the looks of things, she may like words as much as I do.

She brushes off her legs.

"You've got a minor scrape there." I point to her knee.

"Shoot. I forgot my Band Aids. I thought this would be a quick little walk."

I point to the gigantic rock next to us. "Sit on the edge of the rock. I have a few with me."

"What are those things?" she asks, looking at the towers of rocks just off the path.

"They're called cairns. People put them there to say thank you to Mother Nature for the forest. Don't touch them."

I want to tell her she's not the only one on this island who feels like they're one with nature, we all do, but she has no idea she's been emailing me.

She sits down, and I wipe the dirt off of her knee, touching her skin as gently as I can. She shivers and I glance up at her as her blue eyes stare off into the distance.

"You okay?"

"Yeah, I just don't like blood."

"Good thing it's not a gusher."

Her skin is soft, and I catch a hint of coconut, probably from her lotion. I grab a Band Aid out of my pack and put it on. I think she's holding her breath. "There. Not major surgery."

"Thank you. I'm sorry I interrupted your walk."

"You lost?"

"No. I mean, I don't think I am. I'm sure I can follow the landmarks to get back to my car." She looks around at all the trees.

"What landmarks do you see? Because I only see fir trees."

She rolls her eyes. "Are you stalking me? I've watched a lot of *Criminal Minds*, and you keep popping up everywhere I am."

"Stalking you? You've got to be kidding. Why would I stalk you?" That's the dumbest thing I've ever heard. I just put a Band Aid on her, for Chrissake.

"I don't know the habits of serial killers," she chides.

"Maybe you're stalking me." Three random meetings in three days is a lot, even on a small island.

She jumps off the rock and brushes herself off again. "Thanks for the Band Aid. It's been real."

She walks away. The wrong way, if she parked in the parking lot.

"Your car's the other way."

She huffs and turns around.

"And just for the record, I'm not following you. My car's that way too." I keep my hands in my pockets, assuming a nonthreatening stance so I don't earn any other nicknames.

"You had your chance to kill me and you didn't. Maybe I misjudged your killer tendencies."

"You said you've only been here a few days? Visiting?"

Something rustles in the trees and she looks up before turning around and giving me a once over. "I'm not giving you any more information about myself until I'm certain you're on the up and up."

"Like you said, I didn't kill you."

"Correct, but there are plenty of other ways you can harm me."

We get to the parking lot. She walks up to her old blue SUV and turns around. "Moved here from Virginia, Ferry Guy."

It's got to be her. She's the new owner of Applehill Farm.

———

An hour later, I pull up to Applehill Farm and walk up to the porch. I move to knock on the door, but it flies open before I can.

"What are YOU doing here?" she asks, tapping her foot.

I put my hands up. "I come in peace." I offer a handshake. "Josh Sherman."

"Sherman? I met another Sherman yesterday."

"One of my brothers."

"How many of you are there?" she asks, looking around like another one may pop out of a bush.

"Four Sherman siblings. I have a sister and two brothers."

She logs the fact with a shake of her head.

"Anyway, I was working with your uncle on a project before he passed away. I'm J. The guy you've been emailing."

"That's you? Clearly, I haven't been using my best investigative reporter skills." She puts her finger on her chin. "You're Ferry Guy *and* Mr. Grumpy Pants?"

"Guilty as charged."

I put my hands in my pockets and rock on my heels. She's changed out of her exercise shorts and has overalls and a tank top on, with a flannel tied around her waist. It's a sexy look, and a little more PNW than the other things she's been wearing.

"At what point did you know you were talking to me?" Her brow furrows.

"I was pretty sure it was you last night when we were messaging each other, but this morning, when you said you moved here from Virginia, I was certain. "

"You couldn't have asked me when we were emailing or introduced yourself on the trail?"

"Nope. Too busy getting you upright and applying first aid."

She rolls her eyes. "You're not what I expected."

"Not a criminal?" I can feel the corners of my lips twitching slightly upwards.

"No, you could still be a criminal, but I figured one of Uncle Don's friends was taking care of this place. I pictured an old guy smoking a pipe and typing emails with one finger. Instead, you were just being an ass with your short replies."

"Does anyone smoke pipes anymore?" I ask.

"That's beside the point." She sits down on a porch step. "How'd you end up helping with Applehill Farm?"

"I was making a map for Don's Harvest Fest, and one thing led to another and I've been taking care of things around here since then. Maya, Don's friend, has been in a state of shock, so I took over."

She puts her arms on her knees and looks around. "What do you need from me?"

"Someone has to take over the planning for Harvest Fest, and since you're here, it's your job."

"I just got here a couple of days ago. I barely know how to drive on the boat or get to the grocery store from here."

That much was clear when I tried to drive off the ferry behind her. I run to my glove compartment, take out one of the maps I made of Greensea Island, and hand it to her. I keep them there to hand to all the randoms who can't seem to find their way and claim they have no cell service on the island. The map helps them go on their merry way.

"Here. Take a right at the top of the hill. A left on Rhododendron Way. Go two miles and turn right on Madrona. Voila."

"I didn't mean literally. And who has maps like this just hanging out in their car?"

"One of my jobs." I need to free myself of some responsibilities, and this Harvest Fest is the top thing on my list, but this conversation isn't going anywhere. "Okay. When you get your shit together, let me know and I'll tell you what I've already taken care of." I turn around and start down the steps.

"Do you have a phone number, or something besides your email? You don't always respond fast enough. Or should I just assume you're tailing me and we'll run into each other eventually?"

I pull out my wallet to grab a card. Of course, I only have my Party Pirate cards and none of my consultant cards. I hand it to her and brace myself for her reaction.

"Hmm. A pirate." A deadpan response.

"Go ahead. Lay it on me. I've heard them all. How does a pirate get to work? By carrrrrrr. Why doesn't a pirate like to play cards? Because he's standing on the deck. How do pirates prefer to communicate? Aye to aye."

She lets out a little laugh.

"I was just going to tell you I'm a party magician."

"Hmm," I respond. A mapmaker and a magician. Who would've thought? "Call me when you're ready to talk apples."

"Aye aye, matey." She giggles. "Sorry, I couldn't resist."

I walk a couple more steps to my car.

"Hey!" she yells. "Why did the magician bring a pencil to the show?"

"I have no idea," I answer, as I walk backwards to my Prius.

"She wanted to draw a crowd."

"Goodbye, magician."

"It's Sylviane, by the way."

"Sylviane?" I throw her a questioning look.

"My name." She smiles.

I nod and get in the car. Interesting name...I'll look it up as soon as I get home.

TWELVE

SYLVIANE

What the actual hell? Ferry Guy and Mr. Grumpy Pants are the same person. I see it now; both have a sarcastic side. Both are succinct in their responses. Both wake up on the wrong side of the bed every morning. I thought I was emailing someone who had his AARP card. Instead, he's my age, and I've daydreamed about his head lying on my pillow while we discuss literature. He could be my spirit twin, if that's even a thing. How am I going to talk shop with him now?

I walk into the only Mexican restaurant in town, looking for my comfort food—a cheese enchilada with a side of rice and beans. When things in my life feel a little out of control, a cheese enchilada is one of the only things I can count on.

I need a plan. In addition to working on Harvest Fest, which I don't even know how to do, I need to take control of my new life before it takes control of me. Purchases need to be made and the number in my bank account is getting smaller and smaller.

"One?" the hostess asks.

"Yes." Sometimes I feel like my life will never be anything

more than a party of one. I'm used to eating alone, especially after the last few weeks.

She seats me at a table next to the window. The sticky vinyl booths feel the same no matter what coast you're on. There isn't a cleaning product around that can actually make vinyl feel fresh.

Festive murals decorate the walls and fairy lights hang from the ceiling. It has the comfort of every Mexican restaurant I've been to on the East Coast. I snap a picture of the mural, post it on Instagram, and write "Just like home." Beth made me promise I'd post occasional updates to the 'Gram, and I know Nancy checks my profile, even if she's hesitant to admit it.

I'll ask for the name of the manager before I leave. Who knows? They may want to have a visiting magician once a month, just like La Casita in Virginia.

A burst of air comes in as the door opens, blowing pine needles across the rug. I shiver as the cool sea air cuts right through the vinyl.

"Well, I thought I'd find you here!" I recognize the voice bellowing behind me.

"Ryder?" Clearly, the shiver was from his presence and not the air. Dressed in slim-fit dark jeans and an untucked white button down, with an attaché slung over his shoulder, there's no way his arrival is accidental or coincidental.

"What on earth are you doing here?" I ask, staring at the guy who's about to sit down on the other side of the booth.

"You just posted a picture, and lucky for me, after a quick search, I found the only restaurant that looked like it on Greensea." He smiles and helps himself to a chip and salsa.

Stupid social media. I didn't think Ryder paid attention to stuff like that, but it's not the first time I've been wrong about him.

"Yeah, but like why are you here? It's not like you live across town. Or in the state. Or on this coast."

As far as I know, Ryder doesn't have any business on the West Coast. But I could write a novel about everything I don't know about him. He could live right here on this island and I really wouldn't know.

"To see you, of course." He offers a small, kind of apologetic, grin.

"You flew across the country, took a ferry to an island, and just showed up?"

Ryder never checked up on me. Like never.

"Trix, you moved to Timbuktu. It seems a little out of character. I'm worried."

My heart skips a beat at the sound of my nickname, his nickname for me. I straighten up against the back of the booth and try to prove my resolve. I won't melt for him this time. There is no way.

"How do you know what's out of character for me? You only see me in brief spurts."

"We went to grad school together. I'd hardly call that a spurt. I know you think better with a pencil in your mouth. I know you like three Sweet'n Lows in your coffee and you have a bowl of Froot Loops every morning."

Point taken. I flag the waitress. Now this dinner requires a margarita. Ryder orders a Corona with three lime wedges on the side.

"Grad school was years ago. I'm different now."

Ryder leans back against the booth. "I saw you at the beginning of August, and you still drank your coffee the same way."

I understand what he's saying. The move seems drastic. But he's making me feel defensive, and that's not the energy I want to have with me on Greensea.

"Do you know any person our age who wouldn't move to

live in a cabin they'd inherited? I mean, duh, how could I not?" I stuff a chip in my mouth.

"But your family is in Virginia." He sips his beer.

"My family? I'd hardly call Nancy family. Evil stepmother, more like it."

I take a sip of my drink. The first taste of a margarita is my favorite: the mix of salty and sweet and the tang of the tequila. Perfection.

"I don't have a connection to my family like you do to yours. I kind of got stuck with more than half of them. I should have moved away years ago, but staying was easier. Now that I have Uncle Don's house, leaving was the only thing that made sense."

The waitress walks back over. "Have you decided? I mean, it's basically the same menu you had in Virginia."

How does everyone know I'm from Virginia? Was there an announcement about my arrival?

"I'll have a cheese enchilada with rice and beans, please."

"Sir?"

"Chicken fajitas, please."

Fajitas are the flashy item on the menu. Makes so much sense that Ryder would get them.

"I get why you moved out here. I don't understand why you didn't tell me, Trix."

"Because you're engaged!" It's all caps in my head, like I'm speaking to a toddler.

"My engagement doesn't matter."

"It should matter! It matters to Penny. You had your chance with me."

I let Ryder do whatever he wanted for way too long. He thinks it's normal to have a wife and a side fling. Says a lot about what his parents' marriage must be like. Quite an example Sloane and Dick have provided.

"You know I had to focus on my career first. My dad made that very clear."

Ryder always had to be further along; he had to graduate, he had to apprentice, he had to manage the Rome office. Always a reason that sufficed as an excuse for his parents' control over him.

"But you're getting married now. I can't believe we're still having these conversations when you're about to walk down the aisle next month."

"It's a formality to keep my parents happy. Penny is fine with our relationship."

I shake my head. That's just so messed up.

"I deserved to know you moved," he complains.

I want to explain that I deserved to know so much more than he ever gave me, but instead all that comes out is, "You deserve nothing from me."

He's just mad that he didn't get my attention. That I didn't call and consult him. The old Sylviane would have asked him while we were lying in bed together. And I would have let him do whatever he wanted to me. He's mad that I found my balls.

"Where are you staying?" I ask.

"I thought I could stay with you." He gives me his signature smile that makes me weak at the knees.

The house is barely set up for me. Are there enough towels? Are there sheets on the bed in the other room? I haven't lived there long enough to have a guest, but I don't even know if Greensea has a hotel, so I'm stuck with him at least until morning. Different beds though. What kind of person would it make me if I slept with someone I knew was going to get married?

"I'm not sleeping with you." Salsa drips down my chin as I stuff a bite of enchilada into my mouth and close my eyes savoring the warm cheese and spicy sauce.

"Let's just take it step by step. Right now, I'm just here to have a platter of fajitas with my favorite person in her new hometown."

Favorite person? I roll my eyes. His mom must not know he's here. She'd freak out. The first time I met Sloane Rockenbok, the most look-at-me person I'd ever met, I realized it was a great credit to Ryder that his wealth was not his most immediate and obvious trait. Ryder and I traveled from grad school to his mother's tea party at the family house on the river, or "rivah," as people from the area liked to say. I wore my favorite navy sundress from the vintage shop I frequented in Richmond, and a pair of sandals I'd found at Target. Ryder loved the dress. Really, he only loved the way a bra was unnecessary, and that the straps slipped off my shoulders so easily, which had made us late for the tea party.

The river house was a plantation style home, larger than my entire apartment building. As the valet opened my car door in the circular driveway, I tried to remember how to hold a teacup; was it pinkie up or pinkie down? The other guests, most of them women and older than my stepmom, wore fascinators, matching purses, and enough jewelry to be seen from an airplane flying overhead. Ryder, always at ease in any crowd, led me right up to his mom and introduced us. Sloane reluctantly shook my hand, reached in for what seemed like a kiss on the cheek, but whispered, "Never wear black shoes with a navy dress."

I was stunned into silence, and since I was head over heels about Ryder, I smiled and moved on. I still can't understand how, in less than thirty seconds, Sloane decided I was unworthy of her son's love. And so I set out on a crash course to make her like me. But after several meetings and similar comments about the pills on my sweater or the lack of suffix in my father's name, I realized our relationship would never be more than about what I lacked. To Ryder, it was charming and refreshing that I wasn't from his world. To his mom, it was an affront and something she would not allow for her son.

————

We drive to the cabin in silence, digesting our food and what's in front of us. I give Ryder a quick tour and then head to the bathroom. I change into my pajamas, but layer two extra pairs of pants and a big hoodie on top of them. I need the extra assurance—more layers equals added time—to make sure I don't sleep with him. His dazzling hazel eyes can't charm their way into three pairs of pants.

Fortunately, jet lag gets the best of Ryder, and he falls asleep on the couch. I don't need to make any big decisions tonight regarding right, wrong, and carnal pleasure, and I can take off the extra layers of clothes.

My phone pings with a message from Beth.

Beth: How are you holding up out there?

Sylviane: Ryder's here.

Beth: What the hell! There? On Greensea?

Sylviane: Yep. He surprised me at dinner.

Beth: Ofc he did. Came to save the damsel in distress.

Sylviane: He said he just wanted to check on me.

Beth: Is he in your bed?

Sylviane: No, asleep on the couch.

Beth: Good! Keep it that way. Keep that milk store closed.

Three dots stay in the message box, and I can feel the lecture that's about to pop up on my phone.

Beth: I know you and I know you're thinking about it. I would love nothing more than for this guy to be your guy. But he won't be. He has never been there for you. He never calls you back. He uses you! DO NOT SLEEP WITH HIM!

Sylviane: I won't. I know you're right.

Beth: Text me anytime you get the urge. This is your time. He needs to stay out of it. And don't forget HE'S GETTING MARRIED!

I put my phone away and put my head under the covers, hoping I can keep the bats and Ryder away for the night.

GREENSEA GAZETTE

Dear Islanders,

Oh, la la! The new resident of Applehill Farm already has a gentleman staying overnight. First one to get the skinny on the situation gets a beer on me at The Old Owl. Just put it on ol' GG's tab.

The Parks Department has cordoned off an area of the Grand Greensea Forest. "Someone" has been growing marijuana plants in the forest. Although cannabis is legal, it is not legal to grow it on public property...And that much of it is illegal to grow anywhere except a real marijuana farm. The Grand Greensea Forest is public land, not a weed farm, no matter what the local teenagers call it these days.

Do better, Islanders!

XOXO,

GG

THIRTEEN

SYLVIANE

"Look, buddy." I point at Ryder with a spoon when he walks into the kitchen in an undershirt and boxers. Prime seduction outfit.

"Buddy? Whoa, I must really be in trouble with you if that's what you're calling me. Put down the weapon. I don't bite." He takes a step closer.

I back up and set the spoon on the counter. "It's over between us. Done. Not going to happen ever again."

He runs his hands through his hair and puts them on his hips. "Okay. I get it. But how can I help you get settled?"

"Any experience running an apple festival?" I ask, knowing the answer.

"Do I look like I know anything about that?"

I lift my arms up. "See? Nothing you can do."

He leans against the island, and his boxers threaten to open at the fly.

"Keep yourself together." I point to his region.

He rolls his eyes and doesn't move. "Maybe I can help in another way. Tell me about your situation with the house."

"There's no situation. Don left it to me."

"Is there a mortgage?"

"No, you know the story. Won in a poker game. There's no mortgage on the property."

"Taxes?" he asks.

Shit. Good question. I've never owned anything, and never paid taxes on my rentals. I never thought about having to do that with the house. He seizes on my hesitation.

"See, Trix? You don't even know what you're getting yourself into. Taxes on a waterfront property on this island are most likely astronomical."

I look around at the house. It's a cabin. It's mine. Free and clear. I can handle the taxes. They can't be that much.

"I'm going to get a job, Ryder."

"Party magicians don't make that much, Sylviane."

"See, this is why we can never work. I'm more than a party magician. That's my side hustle. My weekend gig. I am an actual reporter for a real-life newspaper."

"A newspaper in Virginia, and you just moved thousands of miles away."

"This island has newspapers too." I make a mental note to figure out the name of the island newspaper first thing tomorrow.

"I just want to help you get settled."

Seems like a genuine sentiment, but he can't be trusted.

"Ryder, I can do it. Look, I have a lot to figure out. I think it's time for you to go."

"Can you at least give me a ride downtown after I put some clothes on?" he asks.

I roll my eyes and grab my keys. "Where to?"

"Just drop me on Main Street and I'll sort myself out."

We drive in silence. I give myself a pat on the back because I finally gave Ryder the old heave-ho. I knew I could do it. I pull into the grocery store parking lot and turn to him.

"Thank you for offering to help. I appreciate it."

I don't have many people in my life. I should be more gracious to Ryder, even though his sole motivation is between my legs.

"Just call me, Trix. Anytime."

He reaches in to give me a kiss and my stomach tumbles and my heart skips. My mind remembers all the kisses over the last few years. I'd always wondered if each kiss would be our last, and now I know this one will be. It's okay if I return it. His lips are so soft, and his hand on my knee is turning my leg into jelly. But I pull away.

"Buddy..." is all that comes out of my mouth.

This time Ryder rolls his eyes.

"We can be more than buddies whenever you want, Sylviane. The ball's in your court."

He gets out of the car, grabs his bag, and heads toward the coffee shop. I throw my head on the steering wheel and accidentally honk the horn. When I lift my head, I catch the attention of someone in an all-white workout outfit. She must be the same person I saw at the grocery store the other day. I never realized that people actually bought clothes like that. She's coming toward me, and I notice a coffee cup in her hand and a very large brown stain on the front of her white outfit. We've made eye contact and I know I'm in trouble. I have to get out of here. I throw Old Blue in reverse, but before I hit the gas, she bangs on my window, leaving me no choice but to roll it down.

"What's wrong with you?" the woman in all white huffs.

"Me? Like right now? Well, my..."

She cuts me off.

"It was a rhetorical question. I don't care about any of that! Why did you honk your horn?"

"Oh. That was an accident. Sorry, didn't mean to hurt your ears."

"You scared the daylights out of me! And I spilled my entire oat milk half-caff vanilla latte on my outfit, and I don't have time to go home and change before barre, so I'm left with the choice to wear this disaster or skip class."

"I didn't mean to scare you. I'm really sorry."

She gives me a death stare that rivals Darth Vader's. Turns on her heels and walks away. I gently press on the gas and drive out of the parking lot.

"Rabbit. Rabbit. Rabbit." I repeat it over and over, hoping it'll bring me good luck. Hopefully it will be enough to change the energy from my unwanted houseguest and the parking lot incident.

I need water. And fresh air. And to stretch my legs. I follow the map my phone pulls up to get to the nearest patch of coast. Water will relax me. It always does.

FOURTEEN

JOSH

I'm late for my morning hike because I had to deal with a delivery of ostrich eggs. We ordered chicken eggs, as we have for the last two decades, but they switched them with eggs that barely fit into our refrigerator. Now we're running a "buy one, get one free" sale on ostrich eggs, and I'm not sure if I should be grossed out or inspired by the number of people who are coming to get them. Maybe just plain thankful. Hopefully, our normal eggs will come over on the 6:20 A.M. ferry tomorrow so life on the island can go on as normal.

This is my favorite trail to get some exercise on. A nice steep downhill. Switchbacks lined with fir trees all the way down. Tree branches acting like an umbrella as the gentle fall mist arrives. The quiet lap of the waves. I can get some quick exercise and escape my laundry list of responsibilities for thirty minutes.

I poke out at the bottom of the trail, intending to sit on the large rock made for a little meditation, but it's occupied. By

Ferry Girl. We're like a cat and a mouse unknowingly chasing each other around the island.

My footsteps on the pine needles must have alerted her to my presence.

"Are you kidding me?" She groans. "Is there no privacy on this entire island?"

"You don't know the half of it." I'm 100 percent certain she hasn't learned about the *Gazette* yet.

"Yeah, I'm sure I don't, but how do we end up in the same spots over and over again?"

I step onto the rock and glance at her. Some of her hair's sitting on top of her head in a little bun. She's wearing a too-big flannel, a white tank top, definitely no bra, and a pair of sweatpants rolled at the waist. Topped off by flip-flops. A well-used paperback with a half-naked man on the cover sits next to her.

"It's an island, so there's one grocery store, one bakery, and one super great trail that leads down to the water but is still near town."

She mumbles something.

"Tough time adjusting to island life?" I ask.

"I just had an unfortunate incident in the grocery store parking lot," she explains, and tells me a hilarious tale.

"Tight auburn bun?"

Sylviane nods her head.

"Must've been Tippy. If you're going to cross someone on the island, I'd pick someone else."

"I wasn't trying to cross anyone! But what's her problem?"

"She's wound really tight."

"It may be *Sleepless in Seattle*, but it's definitely Grumpy on Greensea," Sylviane says.

Yikes. I've left an impression.

"Why'd you honk your horn? What's got your ponytail in a

knot?" I sit about as far as I can from her without falling off the rock, but not close enough to be creepy. Don't need to add that to the list of my descriptors. Somehow though, I wish I were sitting closer.

"Life," she answers, and picks up a pebble and throws it into the water.

"What's your story?" I ask, sensing something other than Tippy is bothering her.

"Basically, I'm trying to start over. I'll give you the headlines version of my life. Mom died during childbirth. Single dad fell in love with an evil stepmother with a daughter two years older than me. Tried to turn our family into *The Brady Bunch*...was really more like *Cinderella* without the prince. Thought I met my prince, but his evil mother kept me, the girl from the wrong side of the tracks, away. Mother's brother, Don, dies and leaves me the cabin. Drive cross country and start over with a clean slate. The one I thought was my prince showed up at Isla Verde last night while I was trying to enjoy a cheese enchilada."

I laugh. "Sounds like you have a knack for running into people unexpectedly."

"I'm lucky like that."

"Did you get all the way down here in those?" I point to her poor choice of footwear. It annoys the crap out of me when people aren't prepared for what they are getting themselves into. I've spent enough time trying to rescue tourists stuck on sandbars with broken oars, no sunscreen, and a lost Sperry.

"Not my finest moment. But once I started, the sound of the waves kept pulling me in, and now I think I might live out the rest of my days on this rock so I don't have to climb back up the hill in these stupid non-shoes."

"Where'd you leave the boyfriend?" I ask.

She hugs her legs up to her chest and wraps her arms around them.

"He's not my boyfriend! He's engaged to a regal French heiress." She groans into her knees.

"Ouch." Engaged but still coming to visit her. Interesting and maybe deranged.

"I left him in the parking lot of the grocery store."

"Close to the ferry. Nice choice. He can leave anytime he wants."

She looks up and gives me a little smile.

"Do you have an occupation other than party magician? Not that that isn't an admirable profession."

She throws a dozen rocks into the water and lies back on the rock. She's pretty. Kind of like a delicate bird with her tiny features and berry pink lips. Her tank top and sweatpants leave a slice of her stomach exposed. I can just make out the dip of her belly button.

"I'm a reporter. Or at least I was, back in Virginia."

"Looking to get a job at the *Gazette*?" I wonder.

"Is that the newspaper here?" She wraps the flannel around herself, covering her tank top and my view.

"Yeah."

"Then yes, I would like to work there."

I wonder if she'll feel that way when she learns about GG. GG tends to divide people. They're for her or against her. No in between, and lately GG's been making people against her with all her passive-aggressive rage.

Sylviane sits up again. "What do I need to do for this Harvest Fest? Is it like a huge deal?"

"Will it make you feel better if I tell you it's one of the longest standing traditions on the island?"

"Definitely not."

"Then forget I said that. It's just a bunch of games in the orchard, cider, everything apple you can imagine. Easy peasy."

"Did my uncle have a team of people working for him, or did he do this on his own?"

"I think he had people. I'll put you in touch with his girlfriend, Maya. She'll know." I run my hands through my hair. "And I can help you."

I hope it's not just a momentary reaction to seeing her exposed skin, and I won't regret saying that.

"His girlfriend?"

She doesn't even acknowledge that I said I'd help her.

"Yes. They were pretty tight. She's having a hard time with his death. That's why I've been hanging around and taking care of things."

"Got it." She nods.

"Were you and Don pretty tight?" I ask.

"Nah. I mean, he sent gifts and visited me a few times. I always meant to come out here, but one thing led to another. I thought I had more time."

"That's what we all think."

Thinking about that makes me happy my parents are out living their best lives, even if it is leaving me in a jam. At least they're exploring the world while they can. And if they hadn't, Jac would never have met Johnny and had the opportunity to live her best life. Looks like everyone's having that opportunity but me.

The clock's ticking on my workday, and it could take her quite a while to get back up the hill with those shoes, but leaving her wouldn't be right.

"Ready to make the trek back up?" I ask.

"You don't have to walk up with me," she insists.

"Well, if I don't and you twist your ankle out here, then I'll have to do more work at Applehill Farm. It's actually selfish of me to offer."

She smiles and stands up. Rolls the pants over one more

time. They are definitely not hers, and I don't mind catching a quick glance of her hip bone. Who knew a bone could be sexy?

We walk up the first switchback, stopping twice to remove mulch and fir needles from between her toes.

"I need a whole new wardrobe out here," Sylviane complains.

"The good thing is you can wear things all year round. Beanies in July. Coats in September. Always a raincoat."

"Fall in Virginia's pretty warm."

"Not here. Dark and rainy from November first to July fifth. This is actually our nice weather." I look down at her feet and notice she's bleeding from her big toe on her right foot. "I have more Band Aids if you need one."

She looks up, surveying the trail. "It's not that much farther. I can make it."

Stubborn and determined, she walks the rest of the way to her car on her heels.

"Why don't I come over tomorrow, and we can make a plan for Harvest Fest?" I offer.

"Sounds good. I'll probably see you somewhere before that anyway." She gets in her car and turns to smile and give me a quick wave as she rolls down the window. "Thank you for escorting me up the hill." She rolls the window back up, pats the dashboard like the car's alive, and pulls away.

FIFTEEN

SYLVIANE

His eyes were all over my flash of skin. Not in a creepy way. In more of an I'd-like-a-taste way. He's been a curmudgeon of the highest degree via email, and when I first met him on the ferry, and then again at the bakery, he threw grumpy vibes. He still does, but I see cookies and milk behind the hard exterior. I mean, he could've let me walk back to the car by myself in my stupid shoes, but he trudged back up next to me. What would Ryder have done? Well, first, Ryder wouldn't have been hiking with me. If we wanted to see the shore, he would have rented a private boat and had it take us to our destination.

Not Josh though. He stayed with me and offered me help. He could've finished the trail in half the time if it hadn't been for me. And I'm glad he led the way, because the view of his butt in his 501 blues enticed me to keep on going.

I call Beth as soon as I get back to the cabin.

"Hey friend! How are you?"

It feels so good to hear Beth's voice, and it's just what I need to clear my head after Ryder's arrival. Beth and I were bosom buddies from third grade on. She was my check-the-back-of-my-pants friend when we were in high school, the one who gave me her sweatshirt to tie around my waist to cover up a leak. Beth's mom bought me pads and tampons, while Nancy conveniently forgot whenever she was at the store. We were tight, and she's one of the few things I miss.

"Beth! I don't know what's going on."

"What do you mean? Are you okay?"

"I don't know! I have a menagerie of men!"

"A what?"

"A menagerie of men. I've never had anyone except Ryder, right?"

"Well, I feel like there were a few others, but you were blind to them because you could only see him," Beth says.

"Well, whatever. Now, there's Ryder, Josh, and Dave."

"Wait a second, back up. Why are you considering Ryder in this menagerie? You didn't sleep with him last night, did you?"

"No, he fell asleep on the couch and stayed there all night."

"Good, because I'd be on the next flight out there if you were hooking up with him again. You know he's—"

I cut her off. "I know. Don't need the Ryder-is-never-around lecture right now. I know he isn't."

"So, tell me about the other guys, Jess and Dean?"

"No, Josh and Dave. They're brothers. Josh is this guy that I keep running into everywhere on the island. I saw him on the ferry ride over, and we keep inexplicably running into each other. Oh! And he likes books, like I like books, maybe even more. He called me Miss Havisham."

"That sounds intriguing. I don't think I've ever met anyone who likes books more than you though."

"He carries them everywhere he goes. Hardbacks, paperbacks—you name it, he has it."

"Wow, that sounds just like you. Okay, then who's the other one?"

"Dave. He must have been Don's handyman. He can fix anything. Like there's brown water coming out of every faucet, and the next minute he has a little camera down the pipe, and it's fixed. It's his love language."

"Plumbing is his love language? I'm not sure what to think of that." Beth laughs.

"No, not plumbing. Fixing things. And there's always going to be a lot of stuff to fix at the cabin."

"Or maybe he's just pretending he likes to fix things so he can spend time with you," she adds.

"I called him and asked him for help. He really didn't have a choice," I tell her.

"And how was that?"

"Scared the crap out of him while he was checking for bats."

"Bats?" yells Beth.

"Yeah, one flew by me the other night. I think they came in the front door."

"Should I be worried? I mean, what kind of place are you living in? Would the health department shut it down?" Beth asks.

"No. Not at all. I'm making it sound worse than it is. It's charming and cozy. It's "Hansel and Gretel" and all the best fairy tales."

"Ha! Maybe it's a ferry tale! Get it?" She laughs at herself and I roll my eyes.

"Hilarious."

"I need more details. What are they like? Tell me about the librarian."

"He's not a librarian. I'm not sure what he is. He's a party pirate in his spare time."

"A party pirate and a party magician? You couldn't write a cuter meet cute."

"There's no meet cute with him. We've been emailing, but I didn't realize it was him. I've been simultaneously seeing him all over, and when you see someone that many times you kind of become connected. He was helping Don with the farm when Don died."

"What does he look like?"

"Black hair. Piercing brown eyes. Looks good in 501s. Penchant for leather jackets and Docs."

"Ohh...Sounds like a rebel."

"I don't get that impression. Crabby, yes. Rebel, no." A rebel wouldn't be coming over to help make apple cider tomorrow.

"The other one? The bat man?"

"Dave. He's tall. Lighter brown hair. More lumberjacky than Josh."

"I could get down with a lumberjack."

"You could get down with anybody." Beth has a low bar, so her dislike for Ryder carries significant weight.

"And Ryder? Why is he a part of this discussion?"

"He isn't. It's only because he was actually here. In my house. And I'm sure Penelope, or whatever her name is, will beckon him back to Rome in no time," I point out.

"Well, it sounds like you may have yourself a little love rhombus!"

"Beth! I'm supposed to be here learning more about Uncle Don and the property—not becoming the harlot of Greensea Island!"

"Speaking to three men does not qualify you as a harlot. And you're not there to learn more about your uncle. You're there to learn more about yourself. To find yourself. To live on your own."

"I just came here to get away from Nancy."

"You did. You just don't realize the rest of the stuff. Part of doing all this is finding someone to fall in love with. It's putting Ryder behind you and looking at the others in front of you."

I do want love. I want to curl up next to someone before I go to sleep, smell their stinky morning breath before we get out of bed. I want someone to kiss me when something good happens and hold me when something bad happens. I want butterflies in my stomach and kisses in the rain. I want love, marriage, and a baby carriage. And I want a family that's mine.

———

Plan for the night: pizza, movie, bath. A Sylviane Special kind of night. I started watching romcoms when I was little and my dad was too busy with work to do anything with me. Nancy and Caroline were out doing mother-daughter stuff that didn't include me, so that left me to entertain myself. *You've Got Mail, When Harry Met Sally, Sweet Home Alabama*...they kept me company. And I need a good dose of romantic comedy right now.

Before I settle into a movie, I google pizza delivery. It's possible that it doesn't exist on this island. But lo and behold, I find a pizza place that just so happens to deliver, but they don't seem to have online ordering. I loathe having to call someone, but I'm left with no choice.

"Greensea Pies, how can we help you?" a deep voice asks.

"Hi. I'd like to order a large pepperoni, onion, and garlic pizza, please."

"A POG. Yeah, we can do that."

"And I'd like it to be delivered."

"Great. It will be there on Tuesday."

"What? That's like five days from now!" Where the hell are they getting their pizzas from?

"Well, Miss Myrtle delivers for us, and that's the next time she'll be here."

"But I want a pizza now. Who knows what I'll want to eat on Tuesday?"

"No reason to get testy, ma'am. If you'd like a pizza tonight, you can come down and pick it up."

I wasn't going for testy, and I just got called "ma'am." I was simply having a moment of pure shock.

"Sorry. Really, I am sorry. I'd love to come pick up my pizza."

"Thanks, ma'am. We can have it ready for you in thirty minutes."

"Thank you!" I hear a click before I can even tell him the name the order will be under.

I didn't want to go anywhere, but clearly Greensea is not a place with a myriad of delivery options.

Greensea Pies is in a yellow shack nestled on the water. White bistro lights hang across an outdoor deck filled with tables. Inside there are only five or six tables and, luckily for me, the coffee lady and her tight red bun is sitting at one of them. I try to avoid eye contact and go right to the counter to pay for my order.

"That'll be $18.78, Miss Sylviane," says the teenager at the register.

How'd he know my name? I know I didn't say it on the phone. Greensea is an odd place.

"Friends, hold on to your drinks. Who knows what the lady who just walked in will do. I don't want her to startle you, causing you to spill everything down the front of yourself."

"Whatever you say, Tip," they reply in unison.

I can't help but look. Tippy's at a table with several women holding wine glasses. She has a pad of paper in front of her and they're listening intently as she crosses things off her list.

I roll my eyes but remember what Josh said about trying not to do anything that will make her mad. So I pay for my pizza and leave. I make a mental note to come back here and sit out on the deck with a glass of beer and a slice when Tippy isn't around.

GREENSEA GAZETTE

Islanders,

Red alert! The bold barista at Troll Coffee House attempted to make the place a bikini bar. Yesterday morning, someone caught her serving coffee while scantily clad in a triangle bikini. The owner says there's nothing wrong with it and that we're holding back her rights. Of course, he'd say that! The line of high school boys went all the way down the street. They made a killing, all in the name of breasts. Islanders? Are you with me? Troll House Coffee is not the Playboy Mansion. We have island standards, and barely legal women in scraps of clothing do not align with our standards.

And while we're at it, there is no official nude beach on Greensea. The people who have kept the myth alive are evil. Poor Ms. Miller's preschool class, which was visiting the park in Grays Harbor, got quite the view (full frontal—don't call the casting agent for Magic Mike) of Mr. Standard on a rock hunt.

*A quick message to any new Islanders: we don't honk...EVER!
Not even on accident. It scares the fish and other wildlife. Not to
mention the senior citizens and young children.*

*Well, well, well. Mr. Clemente will learn to keep his Venmo
profile private unless he wants the entire island to know about
his expenditures. Who's Roxanne? And why did he need to send
her money for a hotel?*

XOXO,

GG

SIXTEEN

JOSH

Sylviane walks out of the cabin in a pair of overalls, a strappy red tank top, and flip-flops. Once again, I'm not complaining about the outfit, just the footwear. The tank top has me wishing the weather in Greensea were a bit warmer.

She looks like she belongs here and also so out of place. Her hair's pulled back into two little ponytails. Pig tails. Whatever they're called. I had to do Jac's hair once when Mom was at a basketball game with Dave, but I never learned the correct vocabulary associated with girls' hair.

"Hey." She smiles, walking down the steps.

"Can't believe it's been a full twenty-four hours since I've seen you." She looks good. Really good.

She curls up her nose and laughs. "Yeah, almost didn't know what to do when I didn't run into you at Greensea Pies yesterday, or when I passed that random painted goat you guys have."

"Ah, the Greensea Goat. You're hitting all the landmarks."

"What's up with the rocks masquerading as a goat?"

"About thirty years ago, someone walked by the rocks and

thought they looked like a goat. So when people asked for directions, it became a thing to say, "Turn left at the goat." The rock became an island legend, and then on Senior Paint Night, one class repainted it. Now, every few years it gets a touch-up from the kids."

"What's Senior Paint Night?"

"One night before high school graduation, the seniors go out in the middle of the night and paint their names in front of their driveways. They usually add a little extra flair to the island, too, like they did with the Greensea Goat."

"Interesting place." She shakes her head.

"It's yours now, too, I guess. This property is as much a part of island lore as any."

Sylviane looks around at all the trees. "I hope I can live up to all the hype."

"You will."

Her hands move around in her pockets.

"I did a little apple picking before you got here. Let's check out the orchard and see what's in the barn." I hope magic elves have been here taking care of everything for us.

"I walked around out here yesterday. The trees have a billion apples on them. I'm not sure I'll ever be able to pick them all."

"One step at a time. We can probably find some help with that part of it."

It's only about ten yards to the trees. Don put a picket fence around the front of the orchard near the cabin, with a little arbor that invites you in.

"I'm meeting with Don's lawyer, Shea, tomorrow, so she can give me more details, I guess." She runs her hand through the leaves of a tree.

"Shea's good. She'll tell you what you need to know."

She picks a leaf off the tree and starts ripping it to shreds.

"Tell me about your name. I looked it up. How'd a girl from Virginia end up with a French name about loving forests?"

She looks up at the clouds. "My mom. She wanted to name me after this." She holds her hand up and twirls around. "I guess she always dreamed of coming back here but never had the chance."

"Now you're living out her dreams."

"Yeah, I guess I am." She has a freckle over her eyebrow that goes up when she smiles.

We walk up to the barn and I pull the big doors open.

"Let's look and see what's here."

Shelves, filled with buckets and containers presumably for apples, line the walls of the barn. I put the rented cider press and the other things I picked up in the city in the back. Half a dozen ladders. Harvest Fest signs. Tables. Chairs. I pull out some signs to make sure they don't have dates on them, only picking my head up when I hear someone yell, "Yo!" at the door.

"Dave!" Sylviane greets him like she's known him for years.

"What are you doing out here with this guy?" he asks, pointing to me.

"Oh, Josh and I are looking at what we have for the festival."

"So you finally introduced yourself." He turns to look at me.

"He sure did. I really don't see any family resemblance. Part of me's concerned you're pulling the wool over my eyes again," teases Sylviane.

I roll my eyes. "Nope. Happy to bring my birth certificate next time, if you'd like."

"I'm a man of the sea, and he's a man of books," claims Dave.

"You make yourself sound like a merman or something. And I'm a beast locked up in a castle," I sneer and put the signs pack in their neat stack.

"Truth hurts." Dave puffs up his chest.

"Well, well, well. What do we have here?" asks a dude standing in the doorway.

Sylviane whips around.

"Ryder! What the hell are you doing back here?" she asks, with her hands on her hips.

"I had some business I wanted to finish up before I left. Just came by to say goodbye to my favorite girl." He walks toward Sylviane for a hug, but she takes a step back.

"I'm not your favorite girl! I hope your favorite girl is the one who's wearing your ring!" She wags her finger at him.

Dave and I exchange a glance and each take a step closer to her.

"Okay. I get it." Ryder puts his hands up. "You're starting over. I just want to make sure you have everything you need."

"I told you the other night—I'm fine." Her fists tell another story, wound in tight balls.

Dave walks up to her and puts his arm around her, and I get a quick pang of something in my chest. I want to peel my brother's fingers off her shoulder.

"We've got her covered, man." Dave glares at Ryder.

"Moving on so quickly?" asks Ryder.

Sylviane wiggles herself free of Dave's grip.

"Quickly?"

She's stepping closer to Ryder, so I jump between them.

"Dude, why don't you go? She'll be in touch if she needs anything." I feel her breath on the back of my neck.

"Cold day in hell before I call you again!" she yells at Ryder.

Ryder turns on his heel and walks out of the barn, shaking his head.

Sylviane turns around to face us both. "I can handle myself with him. I don't need anyone's help."

"Never doubted that for a second. Just trying to be nice," I try to explain, but I can tell she's not in the mood to listen to anything.

Dave looks at me and moves his head to the side, like *let's get out of here.*

"Maybe we're done for the day." I take a step toward the barn doors.

She paces around the barn, looking at the supplies. She takes something out of her pocket: a few rocks that she rubs with her other hand and then puts them to her lips.

"Yeah. I need some space," she tells us.

Dave and I leave her to her pacing.

"What was that all about?" he asks.

"I think that's her ex. She told me he surprised her here the other night."

"Pretty bold to surprise someone on an island. Must not want to be her ex for long." Dave laughs.

I feel the same pang I did when Dave had his arm around Sylviane. Like I'm jealous of the guy she just kicked off her property. But come to think of it, she kicked us off her property too.

I can tell Ryder's the worst kind of frat boy tourist. He'd call and ask me a million questions about how to light a solo stove. I'd be so annoyed I'd offer to do it for him. I'd go over to his rental house, light the stove, and he'd call the next day and ask if I could drop off some beer from the store. The next day he'd want me to bake one of our pies and deliver it. He'd call until I ended up being his personal butler for the entire summer. I know his type. I loathe his type. How'd she end up with someone like that?

"She told me he's engaged." I tell Dave what I know about Ryder and her subsequent run-in with Tippy.

"What do you have going on there?" Dave asks, looking me up and down.

"'Going on there?' What the hell are you talking about?" I ask. "Nothing going on here."

"You like her? I can hear it in your voice. You were about to protect her from that dude. Can't remember the last time I saw you get protective over anyone other than Jac."

"Don't be ridiculous. You had your arm around her too," I point out.

This past year gave me a lot of reasons to feel protective of Jac, after her creepy husband dumped her and went on a reality show. Then Johnny Nickel didn't tell her who he was, and she ended up falling for him. Maybe that's raised my radar for a damsel in distress.

"I don't like anyone. You know all I want is to get off this island."

"For a guy who says he wants to leave, you do a pretty good job of finding reasons to stay right here."

Dave stands at the door to his truck.

"They're not my reasons. Not my fault. I have to take care of everything."

"You don't see me or Ollie getting roped into all the stuff that you do."

Checkmate. He has a point. Oliver rarely comes over from the city, and he could if he wanted to. And Dave can leave his precious sea creatures alone and help at the store whenever he wants to, but he doesn't.

"Come to think of it, you're right. Why do I get stuck doing all this shit?"

"You've always been that guy. The dependable one. The person Mom and Dad could count on to come home before curfew, put your dishes in the dishwasher, not burn the house down when you were home alone."

That's not completely true. I've messed up plenty, but Dave's right: I have morphed into the one who takes care of everything. It was one thing when I was in charge of taking out the recycling, but this is a whole new level of responsibility.

Doesn't matter. I'm going to get out of here and live my best life, and get a handle on whatever it is I'm feeling.

"I'm going to leave the island."

"Yeah, I'll believe it when I see it." Dave gets in his truck and drives away.

GREENSEA GAZETTE

Dear Islanders,

Are we watching a little love rhombus with our newest resident? It seems she's had a male visitor from afar and now may be out and about with two of our long-time sparring, local brothers. We already reported that the lovely lady of Applehill Farm had a gentleman caller who aptly stayed overnight. Sounds like the cabin continues to spin tales that legends will be made of. Does she favor one over the others, or is she just stringing them along to see what she can get from them?

To the owner of the dog who walked around the park with a rubber penis in its mouth: do better. There are children playing there.

Last weekend was the Annual Squash Race, ushering in the last farmer's market of the season. We do believe that the Holloways' vehicle should have been ruled illegal. There is no way that squash was not genetically modified. Rumor has it that Mr.

Holloway, our favorite retired football coach, injected creatine into the squash as it grew. Was it worth it? The squash won but crushed the dreams of all the six-year-olds who participated in the race. Next year, the market will institute an age restriction for entrants in the race.

XOXO,

GG

SEVENTEEN

SYLVIANE

Today is down to business without interruptions from random males. Shea is prompt and businesslike when she arrives. We sit at the table in the cabin and she pulls out a pile of papers.

"Okay. So tell me. This is all mine?" I ask Shea. "And it's all my responsibility?"

Josh explained it to me, but I want to make sure from a legal standpoint.

"Yes, it's all yours. The land, the two buildings, the trees, the chickens, and anything else Don had."

"I know nothing about trees. Or chickens." I wrote an article for *The Richmond Times* about homesteading. I interviewed people who were doing it, but they were trying to subsist only on things from their land. Unless I plan on eating only apples and eggs for the rest of my life, which I do not, I am not a homesteader. And I guess I need to make it turn a profit.

"To be honest, I don't either, but the Sherman brothers can help you. Maya may as well."

Yeah, the Sherman brothers. They seem to be the answer to

a lot of my questions. Even with the grumpy façade, I'd let Josh, and his eyebrows, answer questions for me all day.

I look outside at the water. I've never even mowed a lawn. I place a pot of grocery store mums next to my pumpkin on my porch steps every fall, but that's the extent of my green thumb. It's not even pale green.

"It'll take hours—no, days—to harvest all the apples." This Harvest Fest is stressing me out. Apparently, I have to make cider too.

"Well, look at it like this: it's your job now. You have built-in income. An almost free house. It's life-changing, Sylviane."

Yes...life-changing. Life-changing is a good thing. Maybe it will bring me some luck in love, too. But right now I have to focus on apples. And harvesting them. All of them.

"A friend of mine asked me about taxes for this place. They're probably a pretty penny." This is the one time I hope Ryder is wrong.

"Yes, that's what I wanted to talk to you about next. You'll pay an estate tax." Shea rifles through her pile of papers. "This is a copy of your uncle's accounts."

She hands me the paper, and I gasp. "This can't be true."

$1,000,359 sits at the bottom of the page.

I don't know what I thought Uncle Don had, but it surely wasn't over a million dollars. Maybe I shouldn't be surprised. I didn't know much about him or what he did. But none of this looks like it belonged to a millionaire. I mean, shouldn't he have staff and people taking care of everything for him? Big screen TVs. Brand new appliances. Or maybe that's why he had all the money, because he didn't live that way.

"The value of the house, plus the money he had in the bank, puts you above the 2.7 million you can inherit in the state of Washington without paying any taxes."

"I don't have that kind of money. Can I use what's in his

account to pay for it?" I reach into my pocket and rub my crystals. I thought the house was a gift, and I never thought about taxes. Ryder was right. I should have listened to him.

"There's more to this story. You owe taxes on your uncle's estate, but someone has taken the unusual tact of prepaying them for you. I wasn't able to find out who did it, but since your name is on the will and the deed now, you might if you call the state offices."

Someone paid my taxes. One of Uncle Don's friends must've taken care of things. I haven't met any of them yet, but I'll have to call around and figure out how to thank them.

"Now, the million dollars in your Uncle Don's bank account does not set you up so you don't have to work for the rest of your life. But that, coupled with this property and the earnings you'll get from it, gives you freedom and time to figure things out."

A million dollars isn't enough money? What the heck! I don't need much. It means I can hang up my top hat though. No more pulling rabbits out of hats or blowing up balloon animals in Mexican restaurants. I can write full time. Be a reporter. Find my way above the fold. Uncle Don gave me a gift. I won't have to talk Nancy into reinstating my credit card. I can figure out how to do all of this on my own. Finally, a new life.

———

Shea leaves. I call the city desk first to ask some questions about the taxes. Eventually, I find my way to the Department of Revenue and ask if they can tell me who paid the bill.

"Okay. I need to ask you a few questions to verify you're the account holder."

She asks me about Uncle Don and, apparently, he had everything neat and tidy, because I'm easily identified as the next of kin.

"Let's see here." She giggles. "Oh, yes! I remember a handsome young man came down here and paid for the whole thing. We couldn't believe it. He just wanted it to be put toward your account, like he was paying your bar tab or something. We rarely take that much money in a check, but of course, we did once we verified that there was enough money in his account."

A handsome young man. "Did the person have sandy blond hair?"

"Yes! Yes! And he was so polite. A real charmer!"

The kind lady is very forthcoming with the information. Turns out Ryder had pulled some strings, made some calls, and paid the bill before he flew back to Italy. Freaking Ryder! I told him to go away yesterday, and he went and did this? What the hell?

"Is there any way to cancel the payment?" I ask. I'm not taking his money.

"Well, I'll be! I've never had anyone ask to cancel a payment made on their behalf. That's not true. I've just never had anyone make a payment for someone else. No, sweetie. I'm sorry, but once it's paid, we can't do anything to reverse that. We don't have a refund system for our taxes. Frankly, we don't care where the money comes from, as long as we get paid!" she says with another little laugh.

I cannot believe he did this. Why does he think my business is his business? After the incident in the barn yesterday, I thought he'd be gone for good, but he inserted himself into my life without asking. I should be grateful. Ryder just gave me a gift, but I want—I *need*—to do this on my own. I'm not starting over by being indebted to him. He's no Prince Charming, so why should he try to be now?

I press the call button next to his name.

"Trix! Miss me already?"

"Why did you pay my taxes?" I scream into the phone.

"Calm down, Trix. I wanted to give you something, since you wouldn't let me do anything else."

"This is not your house, or your farm, and now I owe you, which is significantly worse than owing the state!"

"You don't owe me anything. I don't want the money back."

"Don't you see? I have to pay you back. I want this to be my thing. On my own. Nothing to do with you, Nancy, or my dad. Just me."

"Relax. I'll have my lawyers draw up some papers so you're comfortable enough that I'll never ask you for the money back."

"I'll still know you did it."

"Take it as an apology for everything I've done over the years."

He has done a lot. Like the time he said he'd come over, and I fell asleep and left a lasagna heating in the stove and started a small kitchen fire. Not exactly his fault, but if he weren't around, it wouldn't have happened. Or the time I ended up in jail for trespassing on a private tennis court. He got off because of his name, and I got a record and probation. The list goes on and on. But still, he's tainting the first thing that's all mine.

———

I park myself in the office and try to learn more about Uncle Don, like how he became a millionaire. Papers fill the desk. Sorting them seems overwhelming and intrusive.

The doorbell rings. What the hell? Who could it be now? I'm kind of afraid to answer it in case it's Ryder, but when I open it, a woman with long gray braids and a gentle smile is standing in the doorway.

"Don's girl," she sighs. "You're just like I imagined."

"I'm sorry. Who are you?" I ask, wondering if I should pretend to know who this person is.

"Well, I'm Maya, Don's friend." Her eyes glisten with tears and a little sniffle gives way.

"Come in." I open the door even wider. Maya walks toward the kitchen. It wouldn't take a brain surgeon to know where the kitchen is, but she walks with a level of comfort and familiarity. I can tell she's spent a good deal of time in the cabin.

"It feels so strange to be here without him," Maya whispers.

I hunt for words of wisdom or some way to console her, but my silence takes too long, and she talks again.

"I'm sorry it's taken me this long to get over here. It's just still so new."

I still don't have the right words, but I decide to give her a hug. I wrap my arms around her, and she returns the gesture. She smells like patchouli and cedar.

Maya takes a deep breath. "Thank you. That was just what I needed."

"I have so much to ask you," I say. "I'm not sure where to begin."

"Probably with the most pressing thing: the Harvest Fest." Maya grabs both of my hands and squeezes them.

"Yes, I'm kind of overwhelmed by the idea of putting on a festival. I hardly know my way around the cabin, let alone this piece of property."

The scope of the festival has been keeping me up at night, along with the worry that there may be more bats dive-bombing my head.

"Oh, darling, no need to worry. I'm here to help you. There's a lot to do, but I'm well-versed and know all the people we need to work with."

Maya pulls her reading glasses down from the top of her head and takes out her phone.

"But." I stop for a second and think. "Do you feel up to this?" Shea mentioned Maya wasn't up to doing anything yet.

"Absolutely. I can't think of any better way to honor Don than to help put on his festival." Maya smiles and rays of warmth and sunshine emanate from every inch of her. "Now, let's get down to business. Ted and his crew will pick all the apples and leave them in the barn. You and Josh will need to work on pressing the cider." She looks up quickly and nods at me.

"I think I can do that," I offer.

"Edith and her team are working on baked goods. We just need entertainment!"

Entertainment. I thought I might store away my magician's wand, but I'm compelled to help Maya out, to do what I can to help her. "Um, well, I'm a magician."

"Don mentioned something like that." Maya furrows her brow. "Would you like to do your first performance on Greensea at Harvest Fest?"

There must be better ways to introduce myself to society, but it's my own fault for mentioning it. "Umm...I guess I could come up with something."

"Fantastic!" Maya claps her hands together. "Now, onto other things. How are you doing in this house?"

"Other than bats and brown water, pretty well."

"Oh, island life!"

Why does everyone chalk it up to island life?

"You always have to be up for an adventure—especially on this piece of Native summer land you live on," she says.

"Native summer land? What do you mean?" I ask, giving Maya all of my attention.

"Well, years and years ago, the first Americans took their canoes right over here to this bay and made a summer camp of sorts. See, the salmon swim right up here and follow the bay back down there to lay their eggs."

"I'll be able to see them out there?" I ask.

"You bet you will! This place is very special."

Maya looks at me. It's like she wants to make sure I know how lucky I am to be here, and that I understand all that Don has given me. And suddenly, I'm not sure I can live up to my end of the bargain.

"Oh, Sylvie, I can see the worry on your face. Your uncle just wanted you to be happy. You know this gift didn't come with any strings. If you don't like it here, sell it. The only thing he wanted to give you was the opportunity to make your own decisions."

Phew. I think. But sometimes when there are strings attached it makes it easier. Will I thrive under the lack of pressure? Who knows? My mind is in overdrive ping-ponging between worries.

"So tell me. What have you done since you've been here?"

I open the back door, and we walk out to the deck as I tell her all I've seen. The breeze off the water is fresh and cool, like fall is waiting for us just around the corner. On cue, an orange leaf drops from the trees and dances down to the grass in front of me.

This place is nothing like the Virginian suburbs I lived in. There's no urban sprawl. I don't have five Targets, all six miles away, to choose from. It's peaceful and filled with nature. Sometimes it feels like life's hidden behind all the trees.

"This property is magical." She smiles. "It was Don's greatest joy, next to news of you!"

"Moving to a new place is a lot, but so far I like it here." I want to prove I'm going to be just fine. "It will be nice once I get to know more people."

"I'm sure you've found the *Gazette*, so you'll feel you know people before you actually know them!"

"The *Gazette*?" I ask.

"Oh, dear." Maya tugs at her braids. "Yes, the *Gazette*. Our local anonymous gossip reporter who posts in our Greensea newspaper."

Have we morphed onto a TV set of *Gossip Girl* or something?

"Is that an actual thing?"

"Sure is! I figured someone would've told you, or Don would have mentioned it at some point. No one knows who writes it, but everyone has a guess."

"How do I get my hands on it?" It sounds like perfect bedtime reading.

"The library keeps all the articles—print and electronic," Maya offers.

Wow. Print and electronic. Having worked for a local newspaper, I know how valuable paper copy is. This gossip reporter must bring in the bucks.

"Thanks! I'd love to look at local island news."

"Not sure GG is worthy of the title news, but she sure is entertaining!" Maya claims.

Maya walks through the house and back out to her car, a vintage silver Mercedes station wagon.

"See you soon, love!" She waves as she gets into the car and tuttles off.

EIGHTEEN

JOSH

"Let me tell you, Ferry Guy, I've never made cider before!" declares Sylviane. She's in a better mood now than when I left the other day.

I YouTubed the crap out of cider making to see what I could figure out before I came over.

"This machine is called a cider press. We're going to stick our apples in here and squish them. The juice will come out of this little hole and into those containers."

"Are you sure it's that easy?" Sylviane asks.

I give her a glare. She's wearing one of Don's old flannels over a pair of low-rise jeans. Her hair's pulled back into a tiny ponytail today, her cheeks flushed from moving the buckets of apples in the barn. I'm not sure this is going to be easy, but we have two dozen buckets of apples that need to be made into cider, so we have to give it a go.

"Let's start small," I suggest.

I empty a quarter of a bucket into the press. The press looks like a car jack attached to a two-by-four. I place one of the sterilized glass jugs under the spout and turn the jack. I mean press. At first, nothing happens, but then we get a drip and then a small stream.

"It's working!" yells Sylviane. She has a huge smile, like she's actually accomplished something incredible. "Can I try?"

"You can, but it *is* pretty hard." My arm's going to feel this tomorrow.

She grabs the handle and almost lifts her little body off the barn floor. "You're right." She tucks a stray hair behind her ear. "Maybe if we do it together."

Together. I put my hands on top of hers. Her fingers are smooth on top of the cold metal handle. I breathe in the coconut scent of her shampoo. My breath hitches. What is going on?

"You're squishing my fingers," she complains. "Can we just abracadabra this stuff?"

"Nope. Can't magic these apples into cider," I answer.

I thought the "heir's" arrival would mean I was done with this place, but it's meant more work. She's hard to say no to and strangely makes the worst jobs close to pleasant.

Sylviane turns the press on her own until it looks like we've pressed as much as we can from that small batch. I raise the press, empty the rest of the bucket into it, and press again. A larger stream comes out, but I have to stop and shake out my arms several times. Sylviane pulls her flannel around herself as the wind whips through the holes in the barn.

"Is it always this windy?" she asks.

"No, but I heard something about a front coming in," I answer. "We get some pretty serious winds coming around the mountains and down the Sound."

I hear the telltale rustle of leaves. We go to the store in the rain, hike in a downpour, swim in a drizzle. Rain doesn't stop much, but the wind can get dicey.

A gust blows one door open and closed again. I stop with

the cider press and peek outside. It's windier than I realized, and the first storm of the season is always a doozy. After a summer with little rain, the soil is dry and has a hard time absorbing moisture. The trees get weighed down from the water, as they haven't lost all of their leaves. All of that makes for a messy storm with lots of downed limbs. We're used to it on the island, but newcomers are always taken by surprise.

I walk back over to the press and dump another bucket when the rain starts. The metal roof makes it sound like rocks are falling from the sky. The barn isn't insulated, and it might be better to stop before the storm gets much worse.

"Snack time?" I ask Sylviane.

She nods her head. "Absolutely!"

We walk to the doors and look outside. There isn't going to be a break in the rain for a while.

"We're going to have to make a run for it." The driveway is not the quickest route, and if we want to stay dry, speed is imperative at the moment. "Cut right through the orchard and go straight to the cabin. Don't take the driveway."

"Got it." She nods.

I turn off the lights and latch the barn door. The rain is blasting my face. Sylviane almost goes down in a mud puddle, so I run by and grab her arm. She's got those stupid flip-flops on again, so I'm not surprised she almost wiped out.

"Holy cow!" yells Sylviane. "It's like a hurricane!"

I'm being presumptuous in assuming she doesn't mind that I come in for a bit. She shivers when we walk into the cabin. The dampness of the PNW cuts right through. She takes her flip-flops off in exchange for a pair of slippers near the door.

"Have you tried your fireplace yet?" I ask.

"Umm, no. It's only September. I thought I'd have a few more months before I needed to do that!"

"Our warm months are July and August. The other ten vary

just a little. Starting your fireplace in September is typical on Greensea."

Don has an old Russian fireplace with a chimney that extends through the center of the house. It's used as a heating system, as the bricks radiate heat. I go outside, grab a few logs from the porch, and throw them into the fireplace at the bottom of the chimney. It's kind of dusty inside, but nothing too major. I light it and listen to the wood sizzle with the low flames. I love the smell of freshly burned wood, and the crackle makes me feel right at home.

Sylviane walks over to the fireplace and throws a bundle of something in. The fireplace sizzles.

"What was that?"

"Oh, just some cinnamon sticks and cloves. Brings good luck and smells good." She walks back into the kitchen. "I made chili this morning. Thought it would taste good after a day of work in the barn. You probably have somewhere to be, but a bowl might be just what we need."

The lingering feeling of my hands on hers makes me want to stay. All she said was that I was smashing her, nothing about the electricity that was, apparently, only felt by me.

"I'll stay for a bit, if you don't mind. Hopefully, the rain will slow down a little."

The wind's whipping the rain across the water when we hear a thud in the distance. The front coming through is bigger than I realized. I watch the fir trees sway with each gust. Our elbows touch as I reach to help her dish the chili into bowls. Her eyes dart in my direction but avoid looking at me directly. Is she avoiding me on purpose?

"This feels like late November, not September." She buttons another button on Don's flannel.

"Yeah, it's different out here in the upper left corner of the United States."

She's going to need some shoes and clothes. Those tank tops won't last much longer in this weather. Sylviane walks to the fridge and grabs cheese and sour cream, then takes a bag of chips out of the pantry.

"Nothing fancy, but it feels like the perfect fall meal."

She hands me a bowl, and I reach to carry some toppings as we walk to the table. There's a quiet energy between us. When you're alone with someone, it's usually clear if it's a friendship or a spark. We haven't had the time to establish any boundaries other than a grumpy level of sarcasm that's turned into two people forced to work together. But right now, with the fire going, our clothes a little damp, and a chill in the air, it feels intimate. I could reach over and kiss her.

"Tell me about the pirate party business. Is it hard to break into it on the island?"

"No, word of mouth works pretty well here. I made one treasure map for a summer camp and voilà, a side hustle was born."

"How dreamy was it growing up here?" She leans her chin into one hand and stirs her chili with the other.

"Dreamy? I'm not sure I'd use that word to describe it. It feels claustrophobic sometimes. Like everyone's minding your business."

"Oh yeah, Maya told me about the *Gazette*. That's wild."

"Yeah, wild alright."

I start the family history speech. We're an original Greensea family. Sometimes called "Old Greensea." Third-generation Greensea. If Greensea had royalty, we'd be it. My great-grandparents moved to the island from the big city when there was only a mosquito fleet of boats running to different destinations on the island. They started the store, Cedar & Fern, as a place to buy milk and chicken feed after you walked off a boat. It was one of the first stores on the island, built near one of the boat landings. My great-grandpa, Earl, started The Old Owl. My great-uncle, Phillip, founded *Greensea Gazette*—the actual news part of the paper. He was not in charge when they added the gossip column. When the big ferry came, Phillip, his wife, Belle, and their three girls left Greensea for a town in Eastern Washington, far from the big city and the crowds of people they wanted to avoid. One of my oldest cousins, Quinn, came back, though, and Grandpa sold The Old Owl to her. The store, the bar, and my family are what's left of the Shermans' living history on Greensea.

"Wow! Your family's more legendary than this cabin." She puts her spoon down and is just staring at her chili.

"Something else going on in your head?" I ask.

"It's hard to hear about families and things they've passed down through the generations. I wish I had more of that. Until a couple of weeks ago, people in my life didn't do things like that for me," she explains.

"Granted, you've received a pretty tremendous gift lately, but you should be able to count on your family to help."

"Yeah, not my family. My stepmother rules that roost." She takes a bite and then, like she's about to spit her chili out, says, "Ryder paid off the taxes for this house. Pisses me off."

"Why?"

"Because I didn't need him to. I don't want to be beholden to him." She swirls her chili around like she's making a whirlpool.

"It's a gift. And deep down, he probably cares about you. People who care deeply like to do kind things for each other," I point out.

Her blue eyes search my face for something. The cabin smells like cinnamon, and the chili tastes like chocolate. Everything about this situation emanates comfort, but it's like she can't find it for herself.

"I've never had anyone do anything nice for me. Now suddenly, I have Uncle Don and Ryder doing things."

My life has been filled with family supporting me each and every way I've turned. It's almost been too much, where I want to escape the island and find some independence. I can't imagine not having any of it, or just an ounce of it.

"Just accept it and be happy. It's one less thing to think about."

"What's your family like?" she asks. "What's it like hanging out with them?"

"Loud, crazy, always up to something."

Annoying and meddling, but I'd throw down for any of them—but it seems unfair to tout that when she has so little.

She keeps looking outside. The sky's dark, but I can see the layers of clouds moving at a quick clip.

"Obviously, I met Dave. You said you have another brother and sister?"

"Sure do."

"Lucky." She sighs. "I always wanted a brother or sister. Do they live around here?"

"Well, you know Dave lives on the island, and my other brother lives in the city. My sister lives in San Francisco for now."

"For now? Is she planning to move?"

"Probably. She's dating Johnny Nickel." My mic drop moment.

"*What?*" Her eyes grow three sizes.

"Yeah, he rented our parents' house last summer, and they fell in love."

"Umm...Johnny Nickel, like the big-time rockstar Johnny Nickel, lived here on this island?"

She must not keep up on celebrity gossip. "Yep. He was hiding out."

I tell her the whole story about how Jac showed up on the island unexpectedly, and we had no idea it was Johnny Nickel staying at the house.

"Wow, that's so cool. You guys really are famous." She tucks a piece of hair behind her ear.

"We're not, but he is."

Her hair pops out from behind her ear again, and I act on a strange urge to tuck it back into place. My fingers graze her cheek. Would it be weird if I kissed her? Would that ruin things? I notice a drop of water on her cheek.

"Whoa. I'm sorry. I shouldn't have done that. Are you crying?" Way to mess it up, man.

"No!" She wipes her face, and we both look up as another drop lands on her nose.

"I think it's raining in my house!" she yells.

"Hold on."

I run to the kitchen and look through the cabinets for some bowls. By the time I return, the water's dripping in several spots. I find as many things as I can to catch it. Sylviane races back and forth to the kitchen, and pretty soon we have all the bowls and cups on the table catching a couple dozen drips from the ceiling.

She puts her head down on the island.

"Only I would inherit a house with so many problems!" She screams into her arms.

"Trust me, this is nothing." At least the cabin won't get stuck in a landslide or be swept away by high tide but I won't share these stories with her right now.

"How can it be nothing?"

"It's just a leak. Pretty common in these parts." I try to put her at ease.

"And why does this island have so many houses with this many issues?"

"A lot of the houses are old. Very few new builds. You're

bound to have problems with older homes. And the weather, the wind, and the rain, are difficult bedfellows for construction. It's hard on the materials."

"What am I going to do now?"

"You're not going to do anything right now. It's too windy for anyone to get on the roof. The fix will have to wait for a sunny day. But it can be fixed. I promise."

I'll have Dave get a crew out here to tarp it and see what they can do.

"I know it is, but sometimes all the steps feel overwhelming. Like I'm a brand new homeowner on a brand-new-to-me island. I have bats and a leaky roof, and I have to put on a Harvest Fest."

Her eyes fill to the brim with tears as she slumps down on the couch. Too forward to wrap my arm around her? Snuggle up next to her? What the hell is wrong with me? She's a newcomer, a long-term tourist for all intents and purposes. I remind myself that I don't like those people, and that I dream about leaving this island soon...

NINETEEN

SYLVIANE

Freaking roof. I cannot believe this is happening. Are there lemon laws for houses? Can I return something that was a gift? I slump down on the couch.

"You can handle all of this." He sits down on the couch next to me. "I'm right here to help you." He seems like he means it. My issues aren't sending him running toward the hills.

The wind blasts rain against the logs. In Virginia, we'd be cowering in our bathtubs worrying about tornados, but people here seem relaxed.

"So this weather is normal?"

"Yeah, pretty much. You'll get used to it."

Little whitecaps jut across the bay. There's a crack, a thud, and then the lights go out.

"Josh?" I grab his bicep and then let go, realizing I touched him.

"A tree must've fallen and taken out the power lines."

I throw my head back on the couch. "Now what do we do?"

"Umm...We light a few candles or get out a flashlight and chill."

Josh gets up and fumbles toward the pantry, using the light of his phone. He finds a big flashlight and sets it on the coffee table. Because the house is essentially one big room, the light shines on the logs up into the loft.

It's foreign to me, this concept of being separated from the mainland by a body of water. I mean do they have to fix things underwater? When I really sit back and get in my head about it, I feel isolated and claustrophobic. But when I drive around and see the luscious moss or catch a view of a rocky cliff with fir trees sprouting out of it, I can sit in the magic of it all. Right now, I'm stuck—there's no power, my roof is leaking, and I'm stuck on an island with the Pacific Ocean knocking on my door.

"So, do they fix the power quickly here? What's the drill?" I ask, picking at nonexistent nail polish.

"They'll get to it. But it happens a lot here. We should work on putting together an emergency supply box for you."

"Like space food rations?"

If I could see his face better, he'd probably be rolling his eyes.

"Batteries, can opener, soup. That kind of stuff. If you want to eat freeze-dried chicken, go for it."

"I'd add a book light."

"That's a good idea. I've had to hold a flashlight on my chest to shine on the pages. Not the most comfortable."

I picture him sitting in bed with *The Collected Stories of Edgar Allan Poe*, trying to balance a flashlight and a heavy book. It's easy to picture the book, but my mind focuses on what he might or might not be wearing in bed.

"Classics are too big to read while holding a flashlight. And the print's usually tiny." I learned my lesson in first grade, when

I tried to read *The Wind in the Willows* after I was supposed to be asleep.

"I read other stuff, you know."

"Like what?" I ask, giggling, thinking of him with a stack of vampire novels.

"I'm a sucker for sci-fi. Alien invasions."

"Alien romance too?" I wonder.

"Umm....Absolutely not. That scares me and makes me question our collective sanity."

The wind whips through the logs. There's a gentle rhythm between the crackle of the fire and the drips falling into the bowls. I trace letters on my arm to relax myself, kind of like writing in the sand, but I forget that it looks weird.

"Practicing sign language?" Josh asks. His arm is resting across the back of the couch, his fingertips a few inches from my ear.

"It's how my dad and I used to practice my spelling words. He'd make me write them on his arm and he'd guess. Then we'd switch. Nancy hated when he called the words out to me, so we found a quieter way."

"She sounds like Mother of the Year material," Josh grunts. If he had a book in his hands, he'd slam it. "I've never tried guessing a word that's drawn on me."

"Here, give me your arm."

Josh moves his arm off the back of the couch and hands it over. I take it in one hand. I turn it so his arm hairs tickle my palm. His forearm is warm and strong. He must use those plier-like exercise things, because there's not an ounce of flab. It's all muscle. I start near his elbow, drawing my letter slowly.

"*P*?"

"Nope."

"*D*?"

"Wrong again."

"*B*?"

"Yep." I trace an *a*, and he guesses *bat* right away.

"Too easy. My turn."

I push up the sleeve of Uncle Don's shirt. He takes my arm in his hand and starts tracing up from my wrist. He draws a line and I get goose bumps. Not because I'm cold, but because his finger is giving me the feels. It's only a fingertip, a utilitarian part of the body, but I swear I can feel everything, including the indentations of his fingerprint. He draws two more off of that line, and I will my body not to do anything involuntarily again.

"*F*."

"You're good." He smiles.

He draws another line with three dashes coming out of it, and I know it's an *e*, but I say *r* instead. Then an *e*. When he starts with the next letter, *r*, I know he's writing *ferry*. But his fingertip's soft, and the rough edge of his nail feels good on my arm. I wish he were writing the word *encyclopedia*. I wait until he traces the *y* to make my guess.

"*Ferry*," I whisper.

"Wait, I'm giving you a harder one this time." Even though it's my turn, not one ounce of me is opposed to letting him do more.

"I need your whole arm for this one. Take off your shirt."

"Don't you think that's a little forward?" I ask but take it off without waiting for an answer. I'm wearing a tank top underneath, so it doesn't really matter.

He traces at my wrist again, and my bicep can't wait for him to get to it. A very slow *s*, and then a *u*. Two *r*s, an *e*, and a *p*, and I know what he's writing because there's no way there's any other word. *Surreptitious*. My favorite word, and the word that I spelled correctly to win my fifth-grade spelling bee, the only thing I've ever won. I let him trace the rest of the word, because who am I kidding? At this very moment, I'd let him transcribe

Dickens across my body. He's determined and meticulous with the placement of the lines. My cheeks heat up thinking about other places he could use his talented fingers. He finishes and I have to guess.

"*Surreptitious,*" I whisper.

"It's my favorite word. I love how it rolls off the tongue, and normal conversations do not give us enough opportunity to say it. So it was obviously my only choice for a fellow lover of words."

His favorite word too. I look out the window across from the table and I swear I see a star twinkling in a little break in the clouds. I look again and can't see it but I imagine my mom and Uncle Don up there laughing at the good fortune my luck has acquired.

I hear a hum first, and then the lights blast on. The magic of the moment is over.

"I'd better go. Have to make sure the store's okay," he says, getting up and walking to the door. "Thank you for the chili." He stops and his brown eyes drill holes into my soul. "And thanks for teaching me a new game."

GREENSEA GAZETTE

Islanders,

Wasn't that first storm of the season a doozy?! Was it the storm or something else that had Josh Sherman distracted though? Opening the store for late-night hours (just like Cedar & Fern does after every storm so that we can stock up on essential beer and pie), he almost sold Mr. Wheeler a chocolate peanut butter pie instead of blackberry. Now, we all know that Mr. Wheeler shares everything with his beloved dog, Turtle, who is allergic to peanut butter! Tsk tsk, Josh! Keep your head on straight or take a cold shower. The rest of you, be sure to heed the bikers on the road today until the city can clean the debris out of the bike lanes.

Speaking of bike lanes: the new bike lane is slated to go right through the playground. Yes, technically that's a shortcut, but does the city council realize they'll have toddlers running across the path all day long? A three-year-old toddling across the lane is no match for a man about to miss the ferry and be late to work. We've heard the reasons they'd like to have riders go through the gorgeous park with the adorable replica ferry playground, but none of them makes sense— something the council is sorely lacking.

As a reminder, empty your beer bottles before you put them in your recycling. We do not want a repeat of the drunk raccoon debacle on Evergreen Lane. Apparently, Ms. Henshaw had a bag of clothing ready for Goodwill pick-up on her porch, and the raccoons opened it and dressed themselves in her concert tees from the 90s. One raccoon was spotted in a Genesis reunion t-shirt. Another an Alanis Morissette tank top. And a third got their head stuck in a Pearl Jam t-shirt featuring their front man, Eddie Vedder. Even though the pictures of the trio using their little paws to finish the beer are viral, as an island, we should ensure our wildlife does not become inebriated. I cannot believe I just typed that sentence.

XOXO,

GG

TWENTY

SYLVIANE

Josh has a crew of his buddies coming over to finish the cider making. They're in the orchard in their flannels and leather boots, standing around with their sun and salt-kissed cheeks like lumberjacks of the sea. I can barely make out his fingers, but I'd love to invite them—I mean him—inside.

It's weird how easy it's been to get used to his presence. I can't imagine Greensea without him popping up in the most random places, usually when I'm in need of help. I've been more damsel in distress on the island than Wonder Woman, but he doesn't seem to mind.

With nothing I can do about the leaky roof, I decide to focus on Uncle Don's things, which I can control. I can't stop wondering how he made all his money.

Most of the office is taken up by a large wooden desk with an oversized leather chair. I imagined he spent his days fishing or playing pickleball and never thought about him sitting at a desk. But then again, anything could have been possible. There are a few pens, a gnawed-on pencil, and a yellow legal pad with words scribbled across the lines:

Walk - vegetables - call Ann

Nothing important. No clues to what he did all day.

I open a drawer and find a shoebox filled with dozens and dozens of handwritten notes scrawled on yellow legal paper. I flip through a couple of pages, each one dated or numbered, a continuation of the one prior. Some have charts with lists of good things and bad things. Others have lists. Grocery lists. To-do lists. A catalog of exercise routines. I inspect a list of names with random words next to them.

Gisele - donuts Morningside Lane peacock
Trent - horse farm deaf in right ear
Tom - Cedar Fern prefers marionberry to blueberry four
Barb - laugh pickleball four

The list is many pages long, all in cursive and different colors of ink. Not a list he made all at once, but one he visited over and over again. Arrows connect names. Some are crossed out. Others have question marks. A laundry list of hundreds of people. What is this? I set the papers aside and dig deeper in the drawer. I find piles of newspaper articles held together with paper clips. Hmm, they look like articles from the newspaper, the *Gazette*, signed by someone named GG.

Last night was book club at Wine Down. Jess has outdone herself this summer with the new young waitstaff. It's unclear if the Greensea Book Club ladies are discussing books or just enjoying the new eye candy. Do not worry about the men though—they took care of themselves. We like to call it "Dads on the Prowl down at The Old Owl" night. The regulars are back. Jac Sherman is even picking up some shifts. Thanks to Isaac Battlesea for asking her if she will go by her maiden name or her married name. We'll give Jac the benefit of the doubt and assume she did "accidentally" drop a beer on poor Isaac. Just know your drenched lap was all for the cause.

———

They walked the streets. They herded children and goats, delivered milk, sourdough starters, and smartass quips. All while pretending to love kale more than Yale. But really, the thing on most of their minds, their raison d'être, the motive behind paying an astronomical price for land a boat ride away from the rest of civilization, was that they wanted all the trappings of a wholesome life eschewing the normal capitalistic values of their suburban peers while still reaching for the golden ring.

One of the next pages has boughs of holly in each corner.

And that brings us to the events of the season. We'll have the annual tree lighting this Saturday, down at the town square, where we hope all our youngsters are told not to bring any whoopee cushions for Santa's chair again. They can simply be reminded that Santa will not be eager to deliver any toys on Christmas if anyone is up to naughty shenanigans.

———

Thanks to Dave Sherman, our town handyman, we have ensured all the plugs work, and he has triple-checked each string of lights. Dare we have a repeat of 2003! Remember to silence your phones this year, as we can only hope Scrooge—I mean Josh Sherman—will see it fit to get through an entire passage of A Christmas Carol *without slamming his book closed.*

———

The live manger will be Monday and Tuesday evening. The church has worked hard to ensure this year's baby does not have colic. Mr. Reynolds and his donkey have promised not to block the school bus route this year. And the teenagers dressed as Roman soldiers have been instructed not to make children cry upon entering Bethlehem.

———

The bell concert will be next Sunday afternoon. Please sign the waiver before entering the church. The bells have been inspected to reduce the risk of their falling apart midring. Santa will arrive just in time for brunch on the Saturday before Christmas. The club will not be serving orange soda this year. Please do not encourage anyone to burp the alphabet with the remaining soft drinks.

———

Heed the reminders and let us, the people of this island, keep the spirit of the season in our hearts and the stinginess relegated to the ferry line.

. . .

Another clip has similar boughs of holly.

Wasn't that a lovely tree lighting...after we caught the naughty house bird that escaped from Georgie's pocket into the town Christmas tree prompting little Cleo to climb the tree and having to be rescued by Dave Sherman. We're glad all of our island children are now safely on the ground. Let's be honest, is lovely the right word for all the drama that took place? At least the tree is lit, and we can move on to the next holiday event. Hopefully, the little menace won't bring any pets with them to the living manger. I'm told there will be a volunteer approaching each car, ensuring it doesn't contain anything other than humans. Maybe one family will increase their tithe to the church this year after making so much extra work for other parishioners.

Witty gossip filled with authentic island color. There's no other way to describe it. Why'd Uncle Don bother saving it, though?

I open another drawer and find birthday cards, Christmas cards, I-miss-you cards. I open the first one and my heart catches. It's signed Helena, my mom. So is the next. And the next. Each one has a sentence before the signature. *Ted and I can't wait to see you. Ted asked me to marry him! I miss the forests out there.* I sit back in Don's chair. Mourning a person you never knew is hard. I learned early not to write *My mommy is dead* on my elementary school papers. To me, it sounded the same as *I have two dogs and a cat.* It carried a different weight to teachers and classmates. I never knew her. But as I got older, I mourned what could have been. But Uncle Don lost his sister, his only sibling. His loss was immense.

I could never understand why love wasn't overflowing in my life. I thought everyone would dote on me even more because they missed Helena. But they didn't. I reminded everyone of her, and instead of embracing me, they shunned me. They feared the similarities I didn't know we had. So I found love from other people. My friends' moms. Teachers. My volleyball coach. Maybe that's why I let Ryder come and go for so many years—I wanted any love I could get. I was even willing to put up with him.

Under the cards is a pile of pictures. They're yellowed around the edges like the picture I have of the cabin. The first one is my mom standing in front of what looks like a college dorm. There's one of my mom and Uncle Don with the Space Needle in the background. One on the ferry. I take the pile of pictures out of the drawer and spread them across the desk. A map of her life in postcard-sized images. They're both gone. I'm the only living link to my family. My eyes start to tear up, but I know this is where she'd want me to be more than anywhere else. I'll frame them, decorate the walls with their history.

There's one more drawer, and it's locked. Why did he need to lock anything when he lived alone? It would have been easy to make sure Maya didn't snoop. I've only met her once, but she doesn't seem like the type.

There's a key rack next to the side door, so I grab all of them and carry them into the office, trying each one until the lock opens and I find a pile of laptops. Five to be exact. I take the first one out, open it up, and turn it on, only to find it's password protected. Again, Uncle Don locked people out of his private things. But who was he keeping out? And why? I make a mental note to call Maya to see if she knows anything.

Dozens of paperbacks, sitting cattywampus on bookcases lining the walls, catch my eye. *Murder in the Sea Cove. The Mystery of the Christmas Guest. Murder at Darlington Station.*

Mystery of the Lost Key. Man, he loved his mysteries. Every book looks like a mystery. I pegged Uncle Don as a history buff. When he was in Virginia, I remember him taking an interest in the Civil War monuments, so I always thought history was what he gravitated toward. I guess I didn't really know him that well anyway. Some books have library stickers on their spines. I put them on a pile next to the pictures on his desk. I'll find the library and return them.

Newspaper clippings, cozy mysteries, lists of people…Who was Uncle Don, and what did he do with his days? The harder I look, the more complicated he seems.

On my laptop, I pull up my last email from Shea. Maybe if I dig into his finances, I'll figure something out. Who was paying him? I'll use all my journalism skills to uncover the mysteries and figure out what he did as soon as Harvest Fest is done.

TWENTY-ONE

JOSH

Tables and chairs delivered to Applehill Farm. Check. Cider bottled and ready to sell. Check. Don had me working on a treasure map of the property, and I know he wanted me to dress in costume and hand them out. If he were alive, I'd be more apt to disappoint him, but there's something about ignoring the wishes of a dead person that rubs me the wrong way. So Pirate Josh will report for duty during Harvest Fest. Other than ironing my shirt, things are either done or out of my hands.

The weekly family Zoom is set for two o'clock, an inconvenient time for the West Coasters, but the only time Mom and Dad are not busy with their adventures in Europe. Their summer away has turned into a fall away, and I'm afraid it will be winter before they decide to come home. Johnny Nickel changed all our lives when he rented their house. And not for the better, for some of us. Technically, he only changed mine for the worse, but it's not like I'm being tortured.

My phone dings with the Zoom reminder, so I pop open my laptop. I really should go stay at Mom and Dad's while it's empty. This studio apartment over the store might be part of the reason I feel so stuck.

Mom and Dad appear on my screen first. I see a four-poster bed behind them. They're in Switzerland this week. Jac pops up from her apartment in San Francisco. She's sitting in her window seat, and I can see the fog gathering around the Golden Gate. Tough life. Oliver's in his loft in Seattle. Bare gray walls sit behind him. And Dave is on a rocking chair on his porch. If only we knew how prescient the beginning of *The Brady Bunch* was.

"Bonjour!" says Mom.

"Aren't you in Switzerland?" Dave asks.

"Yes. But they speak more French in this little bed-and-breakfast we're in. How is everyone?"

Our routine is to go around in order of age and give our weekly update. We've always been a tight-knit unit. I guess things went astray when Nick left Jac. But after she met Johnny, and Mom and Dad decided they were going to be away for longer, we decided we needed to do this to make sure we were all in touch, even when we were miles apart and living vastly different lives.

"Not much here," Dave offers. "Oyster season is going well. Just chugging along. Had to go over to Don's cabin to help his niece, but I'll let Josh tell you about that. I don't want to steal his thunder."

I roll my eyes. "Not much to tell," I respond.

"That's not what it sounded like the other day when we were at the barn with her," tattles Dave.

"Oh, Josh! Do you like her? Is she cute? What's she like?" asks Jac.

"I just met her. I don't know much about her." I silently curse Dave for bringing it up.

"That's not what you told me," claims Dave. "It sounds like

you two have been running into each other all over the island since she arrived."

"I think I'm going to have to make a trip over to see it for my own eyes," says Ollie.

"Calm down. I'm only helping her with Harvest Fest. After that, I'm sure we'll go our separate ways. She just moved here from Virginia. She knows nothing about the festival, and she doesn't know anyone. It wouldn't have been right to just dump it on her." I don't tell them how much I wanted to kiss her the other night when we were tracing words on each other.

"How chivalrous, darling. I knew we raised you right," Mom crows.

"Oliver, what's up with you?" I ask, deflecting the attention away from myself.

"Same old, same old. Punching the clock and training for my next triathlon."

Oliver completed a Half Ironman and registered to do a full one next year. He's obsessive about the training. Fits right in with his tight accountant lifestyle.

"When is that again?" asks Dad. It's good to hear he can speak.

"A year from now," Oliver reminds us. "In Tucson."

"And Jac, how are you and that handsome young man?" asks Mom. I swear she's blushing.

"Good, Mom. Johnny's flying in tomorrow for a few days."

"Lovely. Just lovely. I do hope we'll see him again soon." Mom giggles.

"What about us? Are we chopped liver?" asks Dave.

"Well, that's what we want to talk to you about." She looks at Dad.

"We're coming home in November," says Dad.

"Great!"

"Fab!"

"Yay!"

"Well alright!"

We all echo in chorus.

"Don't get too excited," says Mom. "We're coming home for the holidays, but we're going to get the house ready to put on the market after the Super Bowl."

"After the Super Bowl?" asks Oliver.

"Yes. We spoke with a realtor and she told us that, in the real estate world on Greensea, the Super Bowl is the beginning of spring. So that's our goal."

"Wow, Mom," says Jac. "I can't imagine not coming back to the house."

Jac's eyes are teary. Mom and Dad talked about this once before, but that was when things were in flux for Jac. They sound pretty serious about it now.

"You'll get used to it. And it's time the four of you put down roots in your own places," Mom declares, like it's a new family ultimatum.

"Where will you two go?" Dave asks.

"We're going on the road!" Mom cheers and we all groan. We've heard this harebrained idea to buy an RV before. There's no way she'll be able to stand to be in that proximity to Dad.

"What about Dad and the snoring, or the plate scraping?" I ask.

"We've been living in pretty close quarters this summer and fall, and we're getting along better than ever. Aren't we, sweetie?" Mom reaches in and pinches Dad's cheek.

"Gross. Stop!" Jac pleads. "No PDA from the parents."

Dad pipes up. "We'll need each of you to take what you want before we put it on the market."

"You're really leaving Greensea?" asks Oliver. "Like you don't even picture yourselves moving back in a few years?"

"Nope. We're hitting the road!" Mom laughs.

"But what about later, as you age and you're not as agile as you are now? Won't you want a home base then?" asks Oliver.

"We'll worry about that then," answers Mom.

"That doesn't seem like a very stable plan," says Dave.

"We'll find a permanent address when we need one." Dad, who has his arm around mom now, tries to calm the revolt.

"Why don't you just rent the house so you can have it when you need it?" I ask.

"Because we need the money to buy our RV," explains Mom.

"Again, I'm not sure this sounds like the most solid financial plan for the two of you." Oliver tries to employ a little role reversal. He's always the stable businessman looking at the most secure possibilities. But he's right: Mom and Dad haven't been saving for years for this. This is a spur-of-the-moment decision. They can't blow their nest egg on a box with wheels.

"Things happen. You can't blow all of your money traveling. Look at Don! What if that happens to one of you?" I wonder.

"Exactly!" says Mom, and I'm relieved she's seeing some sense. "We could go any day just like Don did, and we need to live now!"

"You know that's not rational—" starts Oliver, but Jac interrupts.

"Can we please not talk about you dying? This year's had a huge amount of change for me. That house means so much to me. And to Johnny." Jac's crying now.

"You can't just up and leave Greensea." It's Dave's turn to offer some sense.

"We've considered all the scenarios. The house will go on the market in February. No ifs, ands, or buts about it," scolds Mom.

She has the tone of voice she used to use when we did something wrong. Like when Dave let the hamster out of the cage and lost it on the first floor. Or when I rode a bean bag down the stairs and went through a wall.

No use discussing it with them now on Zoom. They'll be here soon enough, and we can sit down and try to talk sense into them. They threatened to put it on the market this summer, but they were having too much fun in Europe to come home and get it ready. Once they're back on Greensea, they'll realize they can't leave forever. And their plan is too risky. The only upside to their coming home is Dad will be here to help with the store over the holidays. Next to summer, Christmas is the busiest time.

Islanders,

Personally, I thought all was lost and the heir to Applehill Farm wouldn't be able to pull off the annual Harvest Fest. But lo and behold, it looks like the wheels are in motion to make this Harvest Fest one of the best yet, we hope. We hear the PTO moms have taken it upon themselves to create a one-of-a-kind dessert dash. They've promised there will be a color-coded system marking gluten-free, dairy-free, nut-free, and vegan desserts. Red dyes are not allowed, and sugar is to be used in limited quantities. Sounds like it will be a blast (insert eye roll)!

Same old rules apply for the festival. Parking is marked. Be careful not to park in the culvert along Honeysuckle Lane. Mr. Aarons is not interested in towing cars out of it again this year, so he will charge $75 per car. If that's not a reason not to do it, I don't know what is!

Remember, wear appropriate shoes. No cleats or metal-toed boots that might tear up the orchard. Stay away from the cabin, and of course, do not go in the water. Let's not repeat the skinny-dipping incident of '06!

Good luck, Heir! Let's see if Sylviane can fill her uncle's shoes... or if hosting one hundred guests on her property will send her straight for the 7:05 ferry!

Happy Harvest!

XOXO,

GG

TWENTY-TWO

SYLVIANE

The day has arrived. It's Harvest Fest, and I think I'm ready. Josh got to the barn at the crack of dawn to help tie up any loose ends. His Prius may be quiet, but I still heard the tires crackling on the gravel driveway. I peeked out my bathroom window as he walked across the orchard. His pirate sleeves billowed in the breeze, his pants tucked into his socks, and his arms were full of pies he brought from the store. He looked around at the trees and nodded, like he was giving everything his sign of approval, before he disappeared into the barn. My heart hiccupped and I started to swoon before I got a hold of myself, remembering there are more important things to do today than peep at a cute pirate.

My nerves feel wired. My stomach's gurgling like I chugged a can of soda. Everything's bubbling inside of me. What if this Harvest Fest doesn't live up to the island's expectations? What if I ruin Uncle Don's legacy and the proverbial history books of Greensea Island have an asterisk next to the Harvest Fest saying thrived until the arrival of Sylviane DuPont? Maya assured me we've done everything we can. I laid out all my crystals to charge in moonlight, gathered all my favorite inspirational quotes, and picked my favorite for today, the one I have tattooed on the inside of my wrist. "What if I fall? Oh but my darling, What if you fly?" Today I'll fly.

I walk outside to do my final check on everything. The sun's out and there's a slight breeze coming off the water. Tables with red and white checkered tablecloths sit around the property. There's a cider-tasting station, and a table for the apple pie competition. The school PTO has set up some kind of contest to win desserts. Josh is in the orchard now giving it another once over. Dozens of apple cider donuts hang from the low branches of the biggest tree in the center of the orchard. It took a good hour to tie them all up, and it took all my willpower not to eat most of them. This festival gives Nancy's parties a run for their money.

"I've got to try this before anyone gets here." I look at Josh and all the hanging donuts.

"Okay, but just one. We don't want all this hard work to be wasted before the guests arrive," he replies.

"You have to try it too." I'm not going to let him scoot away to the barn. I want to continue the playful banter we had on the couch during the storm.

He looks around. No one's here yet. We have another few minutes before the festival officially starts.

"Okay. Here, let's put blindfolds on." He hands me one of the bandanas that have been tied to a large branch at the bottom of the tree.

He's already wearing an eye patch, but he's a good sport and picks up a bandana for himself, covering his eyes completely. It's hard to marry his normal tough guy costume of leather jacket and Doc Martens with this one, but I can't help but smile at his outfit and his dark pirate chic hair. Without my magician's cape,

I look like I'm a caterer for the event in black pants and a white shirt.

"Got yours on? Or are you trying to pull one over on me?" he asks.

"It's on. Feel."

Josh's fingers glide across my lips as he tries to find the bandana. I fight the urge to press my lips against them. Instead, I take a deep breath. He smells like apples and the cedar of the barn, and I inhale for longer than I should as his fingers find the covering on my eyes.

"Okay. You know the rules: no hands," says Josh. "Ready, set, go!"

I open my mouth, lean forward, and move my head around in different directions to see if I can find one of the dangling donuts. My other senses are heightened since I can't see, and I hear Josh's footsteps rustling over pine needles. I search for a donut until I finally find one. There's more resistance as I sink my teeth into the apple cider goodness. It's like I'm playing tug of war with the tree. I feel something near my feet, maybe tree or maybe boots, and the heat of Josh's body not too far from mine. As I finish my bite, I realize there's another mouth on the other side of the donut. Our lips graze. My stomach lands a backflip. I'm reaching to take another bite when my lips land firmly on his. It's a hundred seconds all wrapped up into two. But he doesn't pull away, like maybe he actually wants to kiss me. I step back and pull off my blindfold and find that Josh has already taken his off. We're millimeters from each other. He's smiling and gives me a soft, "Ahoy there!"

"Umm...I'm sorry." Sorry is always my first reaction but I'm tempted to ask him to take me away on his pirate ship.

"There's nothing to be sorry about." Josh laughs. "Our lips were equal participants. And mine do not have an ounce of regret."

I feel my cheeks turn the color of the apples. I'm frozen in place, afraid to move. The last person I kissed was Ryder. I want to see what it's like to really kiss this pirate standing in the orchard but I can't, not right now. Kisses later, today's only goal is to preserve my family history.

"You okay, matey?" Josh puts his hand on my elbow.

"That was the best donut I've ever had." I joke instead of telling him I can't kiss him, now.

"You sure my lips didn't have something to do with it?" His brows tilt up questioning my claim.

"There's only one way to find out." I'll be careful to avoid him this time.

Josh takes a step toward me, leaning down toward my mouth, but I lean to the left and take a bite of the donut. "No, that's definitely the best donut I've ever had." I tease, hoping it conveys my priorities for the day but intentions for the future.

The first cars pull in. Josh shakes his head and walks toward the barn. I'm not lying. The donut was delicious. The outside was just crunchy enough, while the inside was nice and cakey, apple flavored with just enough cinnamon. Sweet, but crisp and tart too. But even though the taste was divine, his lips held promise, like they were ready for more, and I can't wait till I'm not hosting a hundred people at the orchard to see what else is there. My insides feel like they've been on a roller coaster for days. How am I going to concentrate on my act?

A man with a salt and pepper beard and dressed like the man who greets Punxsutawney Phil each year walks toward me with his hand out.

"Sylviane DuPont?" he asks.

I nod my head and reach out to shake his hand.

"Mayor Nickerbottom. Nice to meet you."

"Wow! The mayor. I didn't know Harvest Fest was that important." Now I'm even more nervous than I was before. I touch the crystals in my pocket, rub my necklace, and look to the sky for help.

Maya walks up by my side and puts a hand on my shoulder. "Dear, the mayor always opens the festival."

"And how do you do that?"

"I pop the first bottle of apple cider and declare the season open." He looks at me like that's the only obvious answer.

"The season? What do you mean? Fall?"

"Islander season. We consider Harvest Fest to be the first festival of the year after the tourists and the summer residents have left," explains the mayor.

Man, this place really does not like out-of-towners, and I want them to like this one by the end of today. I thank him and walk toward the house to check on Tabatha and see what kind of mood she's in today. It's been a while since I've done my act. My heart's a freight train racing to the station and I need to catch my breath. It's not the donut that's jumbled my insides and made me giddy. It's Josh. He wanted to kiss me. He chose me. Because even when Ryder chose me, it was as his clandestine side dish and never his entrée.

Maya's core of volunteers buzzes around the cider and pie tables, and all I have to focus on is my act. Cars are parking all along the driveway. Josh greets the festival goers at a table near the entrance with stacks of treasure maps he's signing with a quill. Dave stands near Josh's table and gives me a wave. Good, there's another familiar face. I have an area toward the barn where I'll try to wow Greensea with my best little magic tricks.

A small group wanders to my table.

"You kids ready for a show?"

"Yeah!" Three little kids sit crisscross applesauce with their parents chatting behind them.

I start with my easiest trick—flowers popping out of a wand. A girl giggles and one boy yawns. I make them each the balloon animal of their choice—eagle, pony, and puppy—before I go for the icing on my cake, pulling the rabbit out of my hat. Tabatha's behaving, in that the top hat has not moved as she waits her turn. I take the hat and let each of them peek inside before I say, "Abracadabra, meet Tabatha!" All three of the kids jump up and squeal and ask if they can hold her, just as a woman walks over to us as if she's been training for speed walking in the Olympics.

"Did you have that rabbit in a hat?" she asks. I know the voice and the stern look on her face. Tippy's exchanged her white athletic outfit for jeans and a yellow checkered shirt, appropriate attire for the festival.

"Yes, she's part of my act," I answer summoning every ounce of my inner strength.

"Are you familiar with laws governing animal cruelty?" Her long red hair blows in the little breeze as she asks. I am not familiar, but I have a feeling she's about to tell me. "In our county, no animal is to be used in any act or dramatization without the help of a trained professional. Are you trained in animal behavior? Do you have your veterinarian's license?"

"Umm, no?" I take a calming breath. I have a bachelor's degree in English and a master's degree in Journalism. Tabatha and I cannot be the thing that ruins Uncle Don's festival.

"Since you do not have all the training required to use this animal as part of your act, I insist you do the only humane thing and cease this horror immediately." She's red in the face.

"Horror?" I ask. I pulled Tabatha out of a hat. She's been out of her cage for less than fifteen minutes. I brushed her hair this morning and fed her baby carrots from my hand. I'd hardly call it cruelty.

Josh beelines over, his pirate hat bouncing with every step.

"Tippy, what's your problem?" he asks.

"This is barbaric behavior toward an animal. This poor

rabbit is being harmed in unknown ways." Based on Tippy's tone, I'd expect her nose to be turned up.

"I don't think Sylviane intends to slice and dice the rabbit as part of her act," he responds in the voice I remember from the galley line on the ferry.

"Well, I certainly hope not, but the mere fact that she is even using a live animal requires certain training and licensure, making this act illegal."

"Okay, okay. No reason to freak out. I can put Tabatha back in her cage." I walk to put her into her cage that's behind the table under a black sheet.

"Do you have the proper documentation to be a petting zoo?" asks Tippy.

I look at her, wondering where she left her other marbles and hoping there isn't a health code violation hanging with the donuts on the tree. "I'm not a petting zoo. Just a girl with a rabbit and a top hat."

"If anyone intends to pet the rabbit, you will be deigned a petting zoo."

"For the love of Pete, Tippy." Josh turns to me. My hero in a puffy shirt. "Sylviane, why don't I help you put the rabbit in the barn for the time being? Last time I looked, there weren't any rules against animals being housed in barns. Correct, Tippy?"

She nods and triumphantly walks off to the pie table, calling someone else's name.

"This island protects animals at all costs. I should have expected someone to have a problem with a rabbit in your act." Josh grabs Tabatha's cage and we walk back to the barn.

"You mean it's not only because she's a little unhinged?" I ask.

"No, most people would have just come up to you quietly and said something, but Tippy likes to be the center of attention. Good or bad, any sort of attention."

I follow him to the far corner, so Tabatha's away from the hustle and bustle. It's dim and quiet in the barn, the sound of the festivities muted.

"Thanks for that." A whisper is all I can muster.

We're about a foot apart, and I swear someone could see sparks bouncing between us. I feel the electricity, and it's not just because we're both wearing polyester. This time there's no apple cider donut to force us to together. It's just his free will that makes him take a step toward me. My breath jumps because he's so close, and I think he might kiss me. Like actually kiss me, without the excuse of a donut.

"I preferred your lips to the donut." His whisper comes out in a deep, sexy way. No quippy pirate lines this time.

His words practically bounce off my lips. The smell of gum —spearmint, which he must have had after the donut—lingers in the air. He leans in. My stomach tingles as his eyebrows tickle my forehead. I close my eyes. The laughter and the din of voices outside the barn fade. His lips take the extra step, and the warmth of his breath and the heat of his body move closer to me. My nerves test my balance like I'm standing in stilettos. I take a step back, letting the barn hold me up. He follows, and he presses into me. His lips are soft. I feel his tongue touch my teeth and then—

"Ahem," says a voice. "Isn't this quaint."

Sort of kiss number two. Ended. This time by Tippy.

TWENTY-THREE

JOSH

"Did you put a honing device on us, Tippy? Why don't you mind your own business?" She can't even give me one quiet moment to show Sylviane kissing me is way better than any donut.

"You're kissing in public, Josh Sherman. That's everyone's business," she replies.

Tippy and I go way back. She was in Dave's year in school. Her dad took over the paper after my uncle. In her eyes, when her dad bought the paper, she was anointed Queen of Greensea. You'd think she'd have given up on all that as a full-grown adult. But clearly she's still the buttinsky she was in high school. I'll never forget the time she cased out the bleachers and made a report of all the kids making out behind them. She took her report straight to Principal Ratcliff. Dave was on the list, the privilege of being the only Sherman on there. Secretly, I think she's always had a crush on Dave, but she won't admit it.

"The barn is on private property, Tip," I add.

She turns on her heel and walks out to the orchard, looking for more exciting news.

"That was embarrassing," says Sylviane.

"Tippy's embarrassing," I say.

"We've got to get a hold of ourselves. There are like a thousand people out there."

"Probably under a hundred. I'm sorry though. I'm not into being an exhibitionist, so I'll pull myself together." I monkey with my puffy sleeves.

Kissing someone for the first time while I'm dressed as a pirate and she's dressed as a magician makes me one step away from joining the circus. I don't know what I'm thinking, but this person exudes energy from every corner of her being, and I'm drawn to her, even though I want to leave the island, I also want to stand around and hocus pocus in the barn or in between the donuts. Her smile enchants me and puts me under a spell making me question all my long term plans. I pull myself together and touch the small of her back as we move back out to the festival for the pie-tasting contest.

Mayor Nickerbottom presides as the judge, and it may be the only reason he's the mayor. As far as I can see, there are no other real perks to the job. I've watched people kiss up to him all year just to get the title of Best Apple Pie Baker. They get a sash and a mention in *Greensea Gazette*, but that's all. Bragging rights can only carry you so far.

The school moms on the island—I know that's not what they're called, but everyone knows who they are—created some race for desserts. The table's covered with cakes and pies I could sell for a hundred bucks. One has four tiers, each tier a different season. It's colorful, and clearly labeled that only natural dyes were used. A pie, made with almond flour and no gluten, has cut-out apple sugar cookies on top. Another cake, with a fondant apple tree on top, is dairy free. One cake guarantees a vegan, gluten-free, nut-free, seasonal surprise in the center. The desserts are beyond comprehension.

Each entrant bid for a chance to win a cake. Winning bidders' numbers are placed in a jar. One mom pulls a number from the jar, calls it out, and the person with the corresponding number runs up and picks a dessert. Civilized in theory, until the numbers are called at short intervals.

Just as one lucky bidder reaches for the four-tier season cake, Tippy comes flying out of nowhere and tries to snatch the cake away. The original bidder tightens her grip, which makes Tippy tighten hers. A back and forth ensues between them. A school mom attempts to intervene.

"Tippy, take the cake with the surprise inside. It's much more suitable for a single woman like yourself," says the lady with the dark brown bob.

Tippy huffs and digs her fingernails in.

Other festival goers crowd around the warring dessert women. Mayor Nickerbottom steps next to the cake and tries to come between the women and the dessert table to protect the remaining items.

"Alright, alright! Enough! Will you two act like civilized people? Maybe donate some money and ask the baker to make you one!" he says, but they're deaf to his words.

He puts an arm out on either side of the cake, just as one person tugs and the other pulls. The cake flies into his face, causing him to stumble back onto the table, which collapses in the center. The two warring cake women lose their balance, and the remaining desserts break their fall onto the table on the ground.

"Oh my gosh!" exclaims Sylviane next to me. "I think Uncle Don is turning over in his grave!"

Not a single dessert is salvageable, and the angry auction

winners are crowding the dessert dash, the moms asking for their money back.

"It's safe to say this will be the first and last dessert dash on Greensea Island," says Mayor Nickerbottom as he stands up and brushes buttercream frosting off his jacket. "In all my years, I have never seen anything like this!"

Dave offers Tippy a hand up, which she surprisingly accepts.

"Tip, what the hell was that?" I ask.

"The whole point was to compete for a cake. I didn't know she was going to have a death grip on it," she says, wiping pie crust off her jeans.

"You could have given up at any point. She was there first, you know," I say. After she ruined our kiss in the barn, I don't want to give it up.

"Dude, I think she regrets it. If she doesn't now, she will when ol' GG writes about it tomorrow," says Dave, brushing crumbs off of Tippy's back.

The whole debacle brings about a quick end to Harvest Fest. Most festival goers are afraid to stick around in case they're asked to help clean up the gigantic mess. I grab a shovel and a garbage can and start the hefty job.

"You'd better sort that into compost and recycling, Josh Sherman!" yells Tippy from her car. It's pretty much Tippy's fourth strike of the day. If she weren't leaving, I'd kick her out with a smile.

"Let her go, man. It's not worth it," says Dave.

Maya and Sylviane clean off the other tables and take the strings off the trees. Sylviane is going to remember the antics and the negatives from this day, but I'll help her remember she pulled off a Harvest Fest no one will soon forget. On Greensea, adding to local lore is more important than anything else. I'm aching to explore our interrupted kiss, but there will be time later.

Dave and I carry all the tables and set them in the barn. The volunteers have taken the few baked goods that are left. I carry Tabatha's cage back into the house and put her in the office, but I don't see Sylviane. No sign of anyone as I glance down the hall, so I take a few steps and find her lying on the living room couch. She worked harder than any islander to make this day a success, something I've never seen from a newcomer.

I sit down and prop her legs on mine, rubbing her feet. We look like a couple of terrible actors, still dressed in our costumes.

"You did it," I say.

"We did it," she corrects. "That was like nothing I've ever experienced. Greensea is one of a kind."

"That it is." I move my hands up her legs. We've barely kissed. I'm not sure how far things will go, or should go. But if we count how many times we've seen each other for any length of time, we're well beyond a half dozen dates.

Don's couch is well used and comfy. Sylviane looks at me and scooches into the back of the couch, hitting the pillow for me to lie down next to her. I move a few hairs off her cheeks and reach down to kiss her. This time there's no nosy Tippy to inter-rupt us. I take my time. My tongue finds hers. My hand grazes her stomach, but she yawns, and I'd rather save the rest for a time when we're both more awake.

"I'm sorry, Pirate Josh," she says, as her eyes try to stay open.

"More than okay," I say.

I map her slight curves in my mind, then I get up, grab the quilt slung over the armchair, and drape it over her. A little sigh escapes her mouth, and then, "I love you, Ferry Guy."

Whoa. I stop. I can't move. She loves me? Do I leave, or should I stay and wake her up to ask about it? Should I pretend it never happened? Few things stop me in my tracks, but this does.

I grab a piece of paper on the kitchen island and doodle a quick Greensea map. On the bottom I write, *Gulls Point - Monday at* 11 A.M., and place an X to mark the spot. I back out of the room on my tiptoes, careful not to make a sound.

GREENSEA GAZETTE

Dear Islanders,

Couldn't you just die?! Did you see the mapmaker and the magician at Harvest Fest? Scratch that. Did you see them before they knew people were there? You know what they say: first comes love, then comes marriage...Old GG couldn't have come up with a better meet cute if she tried. Smacking lips while bobbing for apple cider donuts—doesn't get more Greensea than that! I guess the magician's off the market. Or maybe she's just playing the field. Poor Josh Sherman.

Congratulations to Amanda Willows! Your first time entering the pie contest, and you won. It's also the first time Greensea has had a millennial as a winner. The boomers have already started polishing their recipes for next year. They just need to hop on TikTok to get all the latest tricks of the trade. Are you certain that your crust was homemade, Amanda? Or did you use the Goldbelly online food service?

And then there's the moment of the day we'd rather not discuss: the first and last Dessert Dash on Greensea Island. We hope all involved have learned their lesson. The number callers should never have called numbers that quickly, and for that they should feel heaps of remorse. If games are involved, the rules should be more clear-cut.

XOXO,

GG

TWENTY-FOUR

SYLVIANE

Thank goodness there are clouds and a little drizzle this morning. Not waking up with the sun was glorious. My body could sleep for a thousand hours after yesterday. But my head's playing a game of Whac-a-Mole with my thoughts. I can't tell if coffee will help clear it up or make everything move even faster, but I make a cup anyway and find a piece of paper on the counter. It's a little map, I guess of Greensea, with an X, and it says to meet at Gulls Point at eleven on Monday. So cute. My pirate made me a treasure map.

Interesting. A date? At eleven? Dreamy. When I woke up at midnight, I was covered in a blanket I have no recollection of putting on myself. But I have a vague memory of lying with Josh on the couch. I couldn't keep my eyes open last night, but I felt safe next to him. Every time I'm near him, I have that feeling like when you want one more Dorito, but you can't stop at just one. You keep going back for more. When Josh is around, I always want more, despite being interrupted by Tippy, or raindrops coming through the roof, or pesky walks on trails ending.

If only Tippy hadn't interrupted our kiss, maybe there would have been more last night. Instead, I'm wondering if he uses Irish Spring or Dove and if we'll have a chance to get close again tomorrow. My stomach feels like I'm about to get to the top of a roller coaster. It's that second before I put my hands up and wait for the gust of wind through my hair. I love that adrenaline rush.

Part of me is glad the rest of the day took over and our kind-of kiss became the least dramatic thing that happened. I hope Uncle Don's proud of me, and proud of the Harvest Fest. I'm glad I didn't let my looking-for-love heart mess it all up.

With yesterday behind me, I want to see if Maya has any answers for me about Uncle Don, so I give her a quick call.

"Maya? What did Uncle Don do all day?" I cut the pleasantries and start the conversation.

"Well, he was very particular about his morning routine. He went to a different coffee shop each day. He loved to sit at Apollo and have his coffee on Tuesdays. Coffee stand at Island Grocers on Wednesdays. I believe he sat outside of Troll Coffee House on Fridays. I may be getting them mixed up! He took a daily walk in the forest. And he always had an afternoon coffee at Commuter Comforts down at the ferry. I teased him for being a man about town. He spoke with everyone who made eye contact. Some people learned quickly not to look his way when they didn't have time for a conversation! He went to city council meetings and even watched pickleball games. I always asked him why he didn't take it up, and he said he got more from watching."

"Why did Uncle Don keep all the *Greensea Gazette* columns?"

"Oh, that! Your uncle was obsessed with it! He loved talking to everyone about it. He always asked people a lot of questions whenever we passed anyone on our walks."

"He contained multitudes," I say. "Do you know how Don made all his money?"

"Money?" She laughs. "Oh, honey. Don was as frugal as they come! Even though he went out for coffee, he was a black, no cream or sugar, kind of guy. He was Mr. No Frills, that's for sure. Applehill Farm brought in enough for him to live on in retirement. I don't think he had much of a retirement from his job as an insurance agent."

"Insurance agent?" I ask.

"Yes. He sold property insurance. Not much around here. Mostly off island."

Hmm...Maybe he insured millionaires' properties, but Maya clearly doesn't have a clue about his large bank account.

"Don't worry, sweetie. We'll find you a job around here without too much trouble. Might not be a job as a journalist right away, but there will be something that turns up. Especially after the summer crowd has left. You were so good with the kids yesterday during your act. I'm certain the parks would hire you to work at some after-school programs."

"Thanks. I'll start looking soon." I can't tell her about the money until I know more. I don't want to ruin her image of the man she loved.

Shea's information from the bank listed lump-sum payments from someone named J. Edgar. Like large lump sums. Each deposit was around $20,000. Insurance agents don't make that amount of money, unless he was paid on commission and had a strange payment schedule set up. Googling J. Edgar gave me no information. About a thousand people pop up, and it doesn't help that J. Edgar Hoover is famous. Searching Don's name is a dead end too.

His laptop's calling to me from the desk drawer. Of course it's dead now, so I plug it in and wait for it to charge. Trying to figure out the password of a dead man you didn't know well is challenging. Why a man who lived alone has a password-protected laptop in a locked drawer scares me a little. I put my crystals on the desk and summon all of my good luck energy on the keyboard. I try his birthday first. Nope. Doesn't work. He didn't have a dog or a child. My name doesn't work. Honeysuckle Lane is a no go. The laptop won't grant me unlimited tries, so I think. What meant a lot to him? The pictures of my mom catch my eye, and I know what the password is. Thirty seconds later I'm in. After a cursory scan of the laptop, I'm relieved there's no obvious evidence of anything nefarious. Searching for J. Edgar in his mailbox doesn't bring anything up. His email consists mostly of MLB updates and CNN news alerts. He must've had another account. The document folder is filled with files delineated with numbers. I click on one.

"What the hell?" It's password protected as well. I glance around the room. Was he a spy? What on earth required all these secrets?

I've used up all my best Nancy Drew moves for the moment and need a change of pace. At least I can do something useful, like return all of his overdue library books. If there's anyone else on this island looking for cozy mysteries, they'll be happy I took them back. Wait a second...He liked mysteries, and his computer's locked up like no one's business. Did he commit some kind of crime and the clues are locked in here? My imagination is going crazy. I need to stick to the baby steps in front of me and return the books.

As I approach Old Blue, I hear the chickens clucking. Other than feeding them, I haven't spent much time with them. But they sound closer than usual, so I walk over to the coop and see one of them walking around, outside of the coop. The door's closed and there's no obvious break in the structure. How'd she get out here? I have to get her back in.

"Come here, Houdini. Let's get back in your coop." With

every step I take toward her, she runs away. I zag right. She zags left.

"You've got to be freaking kidding me. Houdini, you're going to be cutlets in a minute if you don't get back in here."

There's a bouquet of corn that was used as a decoration sitting on one of the picnic tables. I think they eat corn? Maybe I can trick her into the coop with it.

"Here, little mother clucker. Here, little soon-to-be boneless wings."

I dangle the corn in front of the door to the coop. She looks at me. Cranes her neck from side to side. Darts left and then right but moves forward slowly. I crack the door open and put the piece of corn inside the coop as the chicken makes its way toward me. As soon as she runs in, I slam the door shut with enough energy to send them all clacking.

"We're going to have to be friends, my little drumsticks," I say and walk to Old Blue.

When I finally find the library, it's closed, because, duh, it's Sunday. So I take myself over to a place called Codmother's that promises to have the best fish and chips in the area. Since I'm not an expert, it'll be hard to judge. I simply want some good old-fashioned grease. And then it's home to prep for tomorrow's date.

TWENTY-FIVE

JOSH

I can't stop thinking about Sylviane saying she loves me. Was it like a friend thing, or did she really mean something more? We'd just kissed, so it has to have meant something more. But love! It's next level. For some reason, I'm ready to lean into it instead of run from it.

She's different from the other women I've dated. Everything seems more real with her. Like I feel all the things, good and bad, when we're together. It's like switching to surround sound from a desktop speaker. Everything is more.

My anger at Tippy for interrupting our moment hasn't subsided. I can count on one hand the number of times I've wanted to spontaneously kiss someone, and the last time I was a junior in high school. I'm a couple of dates and then it's over kind of guy. No one captures my interest. But the tug and pull of Sylviane, the depth and the excitement, all make me want more. Her lips tasted like the future I didn't know I wanted. And, I mean, how many people could make writing the word *bat* on my arm feel sexy? It's branded into my skin.

I'm so preoccupied thinking about Ferry Girl, I don't pay attention to what time it is when I go downtown, and I end up stuck in ferry traffic. Some tourists still come over during the fall. I watch a dad push a stroller and a mom wrangle a toddler. An older couple crosses the street right in front of me and pull out their phones in the middle of the crosswalk to take a picture.

Cute, I think, and then pinch my leg to see if I've left my body. That should annoy the crap out of me, but it doesn't.

I pull into Island Grocers for supplies for our picnic tomorrow. An older woman stops me on my way in and asks me if this is the grocery store. I'm not even tempted to ask her what she thinks it is, with a name like Island Grocers. Instead I say, "It sure is!" and let her walk in in front of me.

My phone pings.

> Oliver: Dude, have fun at the Harvest Fest?

> Josh: Yeah. Why?

> Oliver: Good ol' GG saw you kissing someone…A magician?

I slap a paper into my basket. I'll read it when I get home. Now my jovial mood's been slashed in half.

> Josh: That paper sees everything.

> Oliver: Well, who was it? The girl Dave mentioned?

> Josh: Yes, Don Hamilton's niece. She inherited the cabin.

> Oliver: Nice. Can't wait to meet her.

I wish all the news weren't shared via the *Gazette*. Sylviane doesn't seem like the type to be happy when she finds out she's in it. Isn't anything sacred?

I walk around and pick out a few items for the picnic. I don't know much about what she likes to eat, so I plan to go overboard. I'll grab a loaf of sourdough at Cedar & Fern later for some ham and cheese sandwiches. Some veggies and spinach tortilla wraps just in case she doesn't eat meat or cold cuts. Grab a few drinks. Kombucha, in case she's one of those people. Some carrots and celery, no broccoli because it's stinky and gets stuck in your teeth. Cheese and crackers too. And I'll make Mom's chocolate chip cookies.

———

I walk down to The Old Owl to grab some food before I head home. Plopping down at a barstool, I order up Quinn's famous club sandwich. She does it right, with stacks of toasted white bread, real turkey sliced extra thin, thick-cut bacon, spiral-cut ham, Swiss cheese, a little lettuce and tomato, with just the right amount of her homemade mayo. Comfort food at its finest.

"Hey, cuz," Quinn says, as she walks out of the kitchen.

"Hey! How's it going?" I ask.

"Pretty busy for the fall." She looks over at me and cocks her head to the side. "Where's your book?"

"My book? Probably on my nightstand," I answer. Strange question. Why should she care?

"Hmm. Can't remember the last time I didn't see you dragging around a large tome so you could ignore everyone around you."

Good point. I nod my head.

"Come to think of it, you almost look happy," she says. "Like you might start whistling or something."

"Don't think you have to worry about that. Not going to jump up on the bar and give you a round of karaoke."

"That's good." She nods and refills my beer.

Sylviane would like it here. She'd love hearing the story of the owl, and she'd be fast friends with Quinn. Quinn's a natural at talking to people from her years of working the bar. She's hardly met someone she doesn't like, other than Lindsey's frat bro.

I finish my sandwich and head to the car. The street's pretty quiet. We roll up the sidewalks on fall evenings. I can see the chalk mark on the Prius as I head to the parking lot. Cheryl never takes a day off from marking tires to make sure no one exceeds the two-hour limit in town. As I get closer, I see her standing there with her ticket book open, so I start to jog.

"Cheryl! Please! No!"

She closes her book and looks at me.

"Josh Sherman, you've been here for two hours and six minutes. You know the rules," she clucks, with her hands on her hips.

"Please. I'm sorry. I lost track of time at Quinn's."

"You know darn well you're only supposed to park at Island Grocers if you're going to Island Grocers."

"I did. I promise. Look." I show her the freezer bag in the trunk. "How about you come by Cedar & Fern tomorrow, and I'll have a fresh pie waiting for you?" I say.

"Are you trying to bribe an officer of the law?" she asks.

Shit. She's a city employee, right? Not a police officer.

"Never! I just know how much you like marionberry, and the season's just about over."

She squints and thinks about it. "You're right. I do love it. Consider this a warning, and I'll see you tomorrow."

"Thank you, Cheryl. I won't forget it."

"Being nice looks good on you, Josh!"

TWENTY-SIX

SYLVIANE

We're going on a date. At least, I think it's a date. Maybe it's not. But we're going to a park at a planned time. This is just what I need after Ryder. I'm giddy. Over the moon. Tickled pink. Thrilled to bits.

I mentally take a quick run through my closet, sizing up all my suitable hiking outfits, and realize I don't have many options. Denim shorts and a sweatshirt? Leggings? Definitely sneakers. I settle on cut-offs and my favorite Bucknell sweatshirt.

I'm still nervous when I pull into Gulls Point and see Josh standing next to his Prius with a large backpack.

"Umm, we're going for a walk, right?" I ask, pointing to his gear.

"More of a hike, and a picnic."

Josh leads us by fields of grass lining the water's edge to a path at a break in the trees. We walk up an incline and right by a set of graffitied bunkers.

"Those seem kind of random," I say.

Josh explains that they were built in the late 1800s to

protect the shipyard across the water, and then, during WWII, the fort was used to decode spy messages. This island continues to surprise me.

The path starts as a gradual incline but increases quickly, and I'm having trouble catching my breath.

"Water?" asks Josh.

"No, I'm fine. Think it's just because we're above sea level." I clear my throat.

Josh laughs. "Yep, about a hundred feet above sea level. You should be okay without an oxygen mask."

Man, I'm acting like an idiot. With my luck, he's probably going to use something faster than his Prius to back away from me, or somehow erase the memory of our first kiss.

"We're almost at the top," he offers. "It is a pretty decent climb. I'm just used to it."

I'm too aware of my breathing to make small talk. Maybe once we level off, but until then I'm not going to make my distress any more obvious. Josh leads the way, and just as I think I need a break, he takes us off the trail to a picnic table. I plop down onto a bench and rest my forehead on the table.

"I'm not usually this lame. I'm nervous, and I think it's affecting my breathing." I pull my head up and hope I don't have splinters in my forehead.

"I think I've heard everything now! No reason to be nervous. Want to drop and do the nasty right here?"

My eyes bulge out of my head like one of those frogs you squeeze at the Dollar Store.

"Of course not, weirdo! That's gross, and we're in public!"

"Mission accomplished: you're not nervous anymore."

"No, but I'm freaked out. What kind of person are you?"

Josh unpacks the backpack. He has a Tupperware of cut veggies, cheese and crackers, ham sandwiches wrapped in waxed paper and twine, and a thermos. He's the person who packs a picnic complete with all the food groups.

"I didn't know what you liked to drink," he says, and pulls out two bottles of water, an iced tea, and a kombucha. He reaches back into his backpack and pulls out another Tupperware. "Cookies. My mom's recipe."

Swoon. Hook. Line. Sinker.

When Ryder took me out, it was to the trending ramen restaurant on TikTok. It didn't take any effort. But this took thought and preparation.

"You thought of everything."

The sky sprinkles a little bit of mist.

Josh smiles. "I tried to. So, one thing you'll have to get used to is being outside in any type of weather. We don't cower inside when it's rainy or cold."

"So I noticed. What'd you call it? Fruitfig?" I munch on vegetables while Josh unwraps a sandwich.

"Friluftsliv. Good memory," he says. "I wasn't sure if you were a vegetarian. I have an all-veggie sandwich here too."

"Thank you. No one's ever done this for me before." Nancy never asked me what I wanted to eat. I had the same lunch as long as she packed it. PB&J (grape jelly on white bread with chunky peanut butter), a chocolate chip granola bar, and fruit snacks. What kid likes chunky peanut butter? Not me. I suffered through it until she let me make my own lunch, but I still had to pick from what was in the pantry. Caroline's favorites, not mine.

"It's just a bunch of sandwiches. That guy who paid your taxes must've done something nice for you." Josh takes a bite of a sandwich. "Shit. Napkins. I forgot napkins." He wipes his mouth with his sleeve.

"Ryder did nice things for me. But when you have all that money and staff at your beck and call, it doesn't take any effort.

And that's what matters most." I follow suit and use my sleeve to wipe my mouth.

"Tell me about your dad," he says.

Tell him what? That he let Nancy dictate how he acted toward me? That I got two hugs a year, one on my birthday and one on Christmas? When I graduated from college, I got a one-armed hug and a pat on the back. Research says a person should have a minimum of eight hugs a day, each lasting more than twenty seconds. I could be wrapped up in a hug for the rest of my life and still not have enough.

"He's complicated and also very simple. He was just a guy who went to work every day while his wife, a teacher, got ready to have their first baby. When she died, he didn't crumble. He had to learn how to care for a baby and a household, and to hold down a job. It's hard to blame him for anything I lacked. He just did what he could. When Nancy arrived on the scene, he turned a blind eye. Who can blame him?"

Lots of leaves rustle behind me. Shit.

"Josh!" I whisper.

His eyebrows come alive. "Don't move."

Crap. What's behind me? It's got to be a bear, and I'm going to die a slow and terrible death. My face tenses.

"It's okay. Turn around really slowly," he says.

Great! Turning around to face the animal that'll be the end of me. But I do it. First, I see the ears. And then the nose, and another pair of ears. A doe and her baby. I'm not sure if I'm happier about seeing them or the fact that they're not going to eat me.

I turn around and look at Josh. "They're so cute!" The little dotted faces and velvety fur. I look back again and the mom nudges the baby, and they take off.

I'm shivering.

"Thanks for lunch," I say. "It was just what I needed after Harvest Fest."

"Anytime. We'd better start the walk down to warm you up," says Josh.

Josh walks in front of me on the way down the hill. The trail's wet, and my shoes don't have any traction, so I slip and grab for his back.

"You have got to get appropriate footwear." He snickers and reaches for my hand. It seems natural, and I can't figure out why. And he's right. No matter what the activity is, my shoes don't work here.

The handholding is making me nervous, and I'm sweating. "My palms don't usually sweat like this. I mean, I'm not a good hand-holder with big people."

Oh my gosh, what am I saying? I might jump off the trail and bang my head against a tree. My face is burning, and it's not from the decent clip we're walking at.

"I swear I'm a legitimate adult. I just spend a lot of time in my head, and then when I'm with another person, I say what's in my head and that's not always my best foot forward. Especially lately, because I'm living alone after driving across the entire country by myself. And I do not know what this is."

Josh smiles and squeezes my hand. "It's just two people walking through the forest."

I'm back in middle school again at my first formal, when Sean Peterson asked me to dance. Which actually only meant swaying about three feet apart from each other in a big line of boys and girls. I have that same insecurity. I want to pass Josh a note that says *Do you like me? Check yes or no.*

"What do you have on tap for the rest of your day?" I ask, trying to rescue my inane banter.

"Heading to Cedar & Fern to make sure it hasn't fallen apart. Then work on some, um, consulting projects."

"That sounds fun. I'll have to check out the store sometime."

"What are you up to today?" he asks.

"Going through some more of my uncle's things. I want to make the place my own, but I need to figure out what to do with all of his stuff."

"I can come over if you need another hand."

"I may take you up on that," I say, trying to prove I'm not a babbling fool.

The downhill hike back to the car is much easier than the trek up. Josh walks me to Old Blue and opens the door. He grabs one hand and holds my face with his other hand. I'm close enough to see the mist collecting on his eyebrows. He comes in closer just as a whistle sounds in the distance. We turn to see about thirty senior citizens sidestepping on the roadway. The whistle blows again, and they face forward and high step.

Josh moves back. "And there are the Fit Greenies."

"Hmm...interesting." I giggle.

"I'll text you later."

"Thank you. This was the best first obligatory showing around I've ever had."

I get in Old Blue, turn on my favorite song, "Mr. Brightside," and sing all the way to the library. I have a "first day of school, just hung out with the cool kids" high, even though every time we've tried to dig into a kiss, it's been thwarted. But with Harvest Fest over, and our reason to work together gone, I'm worried he might not be so quick to text or get in touch. I'll need an excuse, a reason to call him. A good one.

———

The library's hidden behind a dozen pine trees. My arrival's announced by sleigh bells tied to the door. So much for silence in the library.

"I've been expecting you," announces the woman behind the counter.

"Excuse me?" That's creepy.

"I knew you'd come by sooner rather than later. Your uncle spent so much time here. I figured his niece would too."

"I found some books he checked out, so I wanted to return them."

"Oh, darling, he was all about those cozy British mysteries!" laughs the bespeckled and graying librarian.

"I can see that from his bookshelves. I'm learning about a whole new side of him on this island," I say.

"I have a library card all ready for you to sign," she says, handing me a pen. "Can I help you with anything else?"

"I heard you have all the *Gazette* columns. I found some in Uncle Don's drawer and I want to read the more recent columns."

"We sure do!" The librarian walks over to a shelf and pulls out one issue of the newspaper first, before she hands me a plastic container filled with the weekly paper, the latest edition on top.

"This is the one that mentions your uncle," she says, placing the single copy on top of the bin.

I carry the bin to a table and sit down. My pulse quickens when I hold the copy of the *Gazette* that mentions Uncle Don.

Islanders,

It was the best of times on Greensea, and oh my, it was the worst of times. We'll start with the sad news, but oh, he'd so wish for us to be celebrating and not mourning. Our beloved Don Hamilton passed away in the aisles of our island grocery store. Reaching for his favorite all-natural peanut butter, he fell to the ground. Surrounded by love and assistance, he did not make it. When you go about your life, ask yourself the simple question: What Would Don Do? He would embrace the heck out of his every day, and be the life of the party with a soul made of gold. Be like Don, Islanders. Be like Don.

And now, on to our happy news: Greensea is gracing the top of all the charts with Johnny Nickel's new hit, "Greensea Gal." We bow down and we swoon. Fairy tales—or should we say ferry tales—do come true.

XOXO,

GG

I set the paper down. Reading about my uncle's demise feels surreal. A small paragraph summing up his life. That's it. There's so much more to him.

I pick up the latest issues to see what's been happening since I've arrived.

"What the hell?" I say out loud.

"Oh dear, you must've gotten to your arrival," says the librarian.

I keep going, taking pictures of each entry with my phone, because there's no way I'll remember all of this when I get home.

The librarian tiptoes over to me with something in her hand. "Here's yesterday's. You might want to see it."

"What on earth? Why are they writing about me?" Someone deep in the bookshelves shushes me. Everything from my arrival, Ryder's arrival, my love rhombus—it's all there in black and white. Are they bugging me? Tracking me? I don't get it!

I throw all of the papers into a pile and thrust them toward the sweet librarian, who doesn't deserve any of my venom.

I get in Old Blue and try some diaphragmatic breathing. Breathe in for four seconds, hold, and out for four seconds. It doesn't help. I rummage through my bag and find my crystals. I want clarity and answers. Someone to explain the nosy busybody. I hold the crystals up to my mouth, and then I have it, a reason to call Josh even sooner than I imagined.

TWENTY-SEVEN

JOSH

"I found the *Gazette*." Sylviane sounds a bit out of breath on the phone.

"Hello to you too," I add. "Yeah, it's a piece of work, that's for sure."

"Have you read yesterday's?" she asks.

"No, not my go-to most days," I answer. It's still sitting on my kitchen table from yesterday, but I haven't taken a look because I've been busy balancing the books for Cedar & Fern since I left Gulls Point.

"Why are they writing about me?" she asks. "How does this *Gazette* thing work, and why am I in every entry since I got here?"

Her voice is high pitched and could almost qualify as a yell.

"You're fresh meat. Why else?" I don't have the answers to what makes GG tick.

"Who writes this shit?"

"It's anonymous. The whole point is we don't know."

"Well, they need to get another hobby!"

She hangs up but calls back a minute later.

"Can I come over?"

"Here? Like to my house?" I try to remember how messy the place is.

"Yeah. I don't feel like being alone."

"Umm." I have some work to do before she can see my apartment, but seeing her again wouldn't be terrible. "Sure. I'll text you my address."

I run upstairs to my apartment, throw all the dirty dishes into the dishwasher, shove piles of laundry into the closet, wipe the bathroom down, light a vanilla candle I got at the store's white elephant Christmas party last year, and thank my lucky stars my place is so small that there's not more cleaning to do.

Fifteen minutes later, I hear a knock. I throw an old afghan over the couch I got from Buy Nothing Greensea and answer the door.

"Hey." I try to act nonchalant, like I greet guests all the time at the spur of the moment.

She's dressed in the same clothes she had on for our hike. Her hair's curling a little from the rain, and she has the tiniest bit of mascara under her eye, like she's been crying.

"Come on in."

We walk up the steps. I watch her take the whole place in. It takes her less than ten seconds, and then she plops down on the couch.

"Is it GG that put you in this mood?" I ask.

"Yeah. It's just reading about my uncle's death, and then realizing I've been living in a fishbowl, that put me over the edge." She sighs. "What the hell is up with that newspaper anyway?"

"How much did you read?" I ask.

"I found some in my uncle's things, but I popped by the library and read the rest."

"Do you know the history of GG?" I ask.

"It has a history? Isn't it just some ramblings put together by a busybody?"

"No, it's complicated." And then I explain. "When the island was less populated, everyone knew everyone. Information traveled as people stepped into Cedar & Fern on the south end, then went to Bungalow Bay Mart in the middle, and then around the island. It was easy to keep tabs on people because there weren't that many. You knew all your neighbors. And it was nice to feel connected. Especially during the Big Dark, AKA winter. You knew if Mrs. Nickerbottom had foot surgery, and then you could bring a casserole over. If Giselle's peacock escaped, we knew where to take it. As the island grew, it was harder to keep track of everything via word of mouth. People tried posting notes and updates on bulletin boards around town, but each bulletin board contained different information, so it was impossible to know everything. So someone —we suspect Mrs. Trout at the middle school—started the column. It passed through different hands over the years. The latest author is a bit unhinged, and the columns may mark the end of GG, but it's still an island institution. Best thing you can do is ignore it."

Nothing good has ever come from spending any time on what GG says. It'll all be forgotten with the newest island scandal.

"The origin of the whole thing is kind of cozy and cute. But they're writing about me. I'm mentioned so many times!"

She's alternating between rubbing the stone around her neck and playing with the frayed edges of the sleeve of her sweatshirt. It's easy to tell when she's upset by the amount of fidgeting she's doing.

"At least I finally understand why people I've never met before have been calling me by my first name since I got here."

"That would definitely be a little unnerving."

GG has been a thing for my entire life. I can't imagine what it feels like to step into it.

"I just want to tuck in at the cabin and never leave. I don't want anyone to write a newspaper article on how many boxes of tampons I buy."

"Never heard of GG reporting on that," I say.

"There's a first time for everything, and before you know it, they'll be commenting on my unusual habit of eating elbow macaroni with honey mustard dressing on it." She's out of breath.

"They might report on that, because it's record breaking in its disgustingness."

I reach over and touch her wrist. She doesn't flinch or pull away, so I scoot closer.

"It's an annoyance," I explain. "GG outed Johnny Nickel when he was staying at our house. He had to take off in a helicopter because it caused such an uproar."

"Why'd they do that?" she asks.

"I don't think they meant to cause any harm. But sometimes what they report does anyway."

"How do they get all the information?"

"No idea. I don't know if it's a team working on it or just one person. That's never been clear."

My fingers trace invisible circles just above her wrist.

"It can't be that hard to figure out who it is." Her brow furrows like she's about to accept a secret mission.

"Truthfully, no one wants to. GG's an island institution. Islanders love to hate it. Everyone knows if we figure out who it is, it'll ruin the fun and go away. No one wants that."

She shakes her head. "Islanders are messed up."

Touching her anywhere takes every bit of concentration, because I want to rip her clothes off without any segue.

"What's your favorite color?" She makes an abrupt change of subject.

"Black." I thought that was obvious.

She rolls her eyes. "Black's a shade, not a color. Try again."

I look around and catch sight of the comforter on my bed. "I love a nice crimson. You?"

"Yellow. I love everything yellow. Daisies. Daffodils. Sunflowers. The sun, of course." She smirks when she says it. "Lemons, bees, you name it. If it's yellow, I love it."

"School buses?" I test her theory.

"Of course! Well, as an adult, because as soon as you hear them approach, you hear the laughter inside. As a kid, they saved me from my house."

Her childhood must've been desperately sad and a sharp contrast from the chaotic life of a family with four kids.

"Favorite food?"

I wanted to get past first base, and she's put on her journalist cap. "Club sandwich. What's with the questions?"

"This." She points between the two of us. "Feels like it's about to turn into something. I want to know more about you before it does."

I like the sound of that, so I take a deep breath, ready to answer anything she throws at me.

"And knowing my favorite color and food will help?"

I move the circles to her leg. She scooches a little closer.

"It's a start. I like movie popcorn," she says, with her face an inch away from mine.

"Of course, you like everything yellow," I whisper, glad I took a second to brush my teeth.

"I'm consistent."

I lean in for a kiss, confident we won't be interrupted now. My weight pushes her into the corner of the couch. Her tongue makes the first move as my hand glides over her hip.

"This okay?" I ask.

"Dog or cat?" she responds.

"Dog, definitely dog." The words come out as a grunt.

"Yes, this is okay."

Her hand reaches under my shirt. My abs tighten at the touch of her fingertips. I run mine across her stomach, drawing an X.

"Are we playing the word game?" she asks.

I don't think I could concentrate enough to write full words.

"No," I breathe into her. "Absolutely not. Just marking my favorite spot."

I stop and reach for her hand to walk over to my bed. She slides her sweatshirt over her head to reveal her tank top, which I swear will be the end of me. A tank top, no bra, just her. She unbuttons my shirt, and I take care of my jeans. She lies down on the bed, and I make a mental map of all of her ins and outs. A mole on her shoulder. A scar on her knee.

I lie on my side with my head leaning down to kiss her. She pushes me back and sits on top of me. I could explode—in all the ways—and I can't help but stare right into her blue eyes and let her do whatever she wants with me.

She may be more out of breath than she was on our hike and falls asleep as I catch my own breath next to her. I'm not the kind of guy to sleep around. This isn't a thing I do on a random Monday. She's giving me a new love for the island and my everyday life. I feel like a cheesy greeting card oozing out all this positivity.

Sylviane tosses in her sleep and mumbles, "Map me."

My laugh shakes the bed enough to wake her up.

"You sleep talk, you know." I brush the hairs off her forehead and watch her eyes get wide.

"No, I don't."

"Yeah, you do. This isn't the first time either." We're both on our sides facing each other.

"I've never slept with you before. Are you breaking into the cabin and watching me while I sleep?"

"After Harvest Fest, when you fell asleep on the couch."

She crinkles up her nose. "What did I say?"

"I'm not sure I should tell you."

She sits straight up. "How could you not tell me? Is it that bad? Was I inappropriate?"

"No, no." I sit up next to her. "You said you loved me."

She pulls the covers over her head. "I am so embarrassing!"

"Don't worry, I won't hold you to it." I take the covers off her head and let my tongue do the talking.

An hour after she leaves, my phone pings.

> Sylviane: I'm gaga. Over the moon. Head over heels. Ferry Guy is top-tier. Kind, smart, and hot. Everything I could want.

> Sylviane: Shit! That was not for you!

I text back.

> Josh: Ferry Girl changes everything.

GREENSEA GAZETTE

The Fit Greenies got quite a treat when they came upon our newest resident with one of the Royal Shermans at Gulls Point. A little tonsil hockey, was it? Maybe the heir had something in her eye. Anything is possible, but one thing is for sure: those two are spending more and more time together.

The state will continue work on the new salmon bridge through the fall. We only hope the state will devote as much money to other pressing concerns as they've devoted to the salmon. Knocking down a bridge, widening a creek, rebuilding the bridge...all for a little pink fish that may (or may not) return to the creek and then end up on your plate for dinner. This gossip columnist is almost tempted to digging into this issue a little more to see what exactly is goin on with the Save the Salmon campaign in the state.

Please note that Cathy at Grays Bay Coffee accidentally made a picture of the Virgin Mary in a latte. Grays Bay Coffee is a *nondenominational shop and does not promote one religion over another.*

XOXO,

GG

TWENTY-EIGHT

SYLVIANE

Tasks for the day: avoid embarrassing texts, try to stop daydreaming about Josh's fingers and my undoing, and figure out how my uncle made his money. Yesterday was dreamy. I hadn't been with anyone other than Ryder since grad school, and this was electric and scary in all the right ways. For his tough exterior, Josh is gentle and kind. I mean, he lives over his parents' store so he can help out whenever he's needed. Not many people are that loyal or generous. He helped keep things going when Uncle Don died. He's one of those people who does the right thing, even when no one's looking. But that's all eclipsed by his kisses, his overly strong forearms, the eyebrows that tingle wherever they end up.

I open my horoscope to stop my daydreaming and start my day.

The radiance of celestial favor is in your future as the stars align to shower you with good luck and positive energy.

That's a horoscope I'll get on board with any day. Obviously, it started yesterday with my little rendezvous with Josh. But now I need some luck cracking the mystery of Uncle Don. I want to know how he got the money before I inherit it. I mean, what if he got it by taking advantage of someone, or by doing something sketchy? Do I still want it? Or will I need to make the money good somehow? With all these questions lingering in my head, I need to know how he got it.

I run my fingers across the books on the bookshelf. He was a collector, that's for sure. There are at least a dozen by the same author, H. H. Whitaker. I pluck *Mystery at Dolphin Bay* off the shelf, grab a blanket, and go sit on the deck. The sun doesn't really hit the deck to warm it up, so I wrap the blanket around my shoulders. Little duck-like things, with white chests almost like penguins, pop up out of the water and glide across it like they're running. I could sit here all day.

The dedication in the book reads *To the Lady of the Forest.* Cute. Uncle Don must've felt like he had a lot in common with the author.

The tall pines blow in the sea breeze. The leaves rustle as I walk the trail. A bigger gust comes through and blows the leaves away, exposing a nose.

Gross. And weird. Does this book take place on a make-believe Greensea?

I flip over to the back cover for a quick description. The protagonist is a twentysomething female who lives somewhere in this quadrant of the world. From the back matter, it's hard to tell whether the story takes place in the United States or Canada. I'll have to read more to see why Don liked it.

Two hours later, I slam the book on my chair. Never saw that ending coming. Helena, an unsuspecting grad student, stumbles across a body. Through her uncanny interview and deduction skills, she's able to piece together what happened.

I can see why Don has an entire set of these books. The first paragraph drew me right in. The plucky heroine with my mom's name is so smart. Part of me wants to grab the next one off the shelf, but my phone rings before I can.

"Hey, Sylviane. It's Shea. Do you have a minute?"

"Yes, of course."

"I got a call from someone who was looking for Don's next of kin. Are you okay if I give them your email address?"

"Sure! You don't have to ask."

"Well, technically, I need to ask. But I'm glad to know you don't object," Shea says.

"No prob. Send them my way!"

An hour later, an email from Thomas Bartholomew is in my mailbox.

Sylviane,

My sincere condolences. Your uncle was a stand-up man whom I've had the privilege to work with for many years. I'd like to talk to you about a project he was working on. We need to come to some resolution to move forward. If you could call me at your earliest convenience, I'd appreciate it.

Thank you,

Thomas Bartholomew

My inner Sherlock Holmes can't dial fast enough.

"Hello?" says a deep voice.

"Mr. Bartholomew?" I ask.

"Yes?"

"This is Sylviane, Don Hamilton's niece."

"Oh, great. Great. So glad to hear from you so quickly."

"Well, I'm anxious to learn everything I can about my uncle. The little I know has surprised me, and I still have so many more questions."

"Before we go any further, it was important to your uncle to maintain anonymity."

"Just tell me, was he doing something illegal?"

"No, quite the opposite. He just didn't want any recognition for his work. He wanted to hang out on the farm and move around the island without people bugging him."

"Now you've got me intrigued! What on earth was he doing?"

"It might be a let down when I tell you. Nothing crazy, and probably nothing that would have garnered that much attention, but he was interested in keeping as low a profile as possible."

"I'm at the edge of my seat. What did he do?" I ask, pacing back and forth on the deck.

"He wrote a series of cozy mysteries. Twenty-five books to be exact."

"What?! No way!" My voice echoes across the bay. That's so weird. I wonder if he wrote some of the ones he has on his shelf. "What were some titles?"

"Let's see. *The Enigma at Emerald Bay. Raindrops in Cascade Cove. Secrets in Salty Shadows.* Just to name a few."

"Was one of them *Mystery at Dolphin Bay?*"

"Indeed. That was his first book."

Holy shit. Uncle Don wrote the book I just read. It makes so much sense now. Helena, the protagonist, is my mom. He immortalized her in his books.

"Why on earth did he want to remain anonymous?"

"To be honest, I think he just never wanted to talk about himself. He was silent when it came to personal details. Over the years, I've only figured out the most basic things. I knew he had a niece somewhere out there, and I did a little digging on my own and learned what happened to his sister, your mother. I think he loved to write, and he simply didn't want to talk about any part of his personal life. Writing under a pen name allowed him that freedom."

"That's insane. What now? Was he in the process of writing a book? Can we let the cat out of the bag?"

"He was under contract, and his next book has been edited and now awaits his edits. And that's why I wanted to speak with you," he says.

I'm wearing a hole in the back deck now with my pacing.

"Me? How can I help?"

"I understand you're a journalist. You have an undergrad degree in English and a grad degree in Journalism, correct?"

"Yes." Creepy that he knows that already.

"I've read several of your articles, and I think, with a little help, you could take over your uncle's series."

"Me? Write cozy mysteries? I write fifteen hundred-word articles, not novels."

"Yes, but cozy mysteries are formulaic, and I'm certain, with some work, you could figure it out."

"I don't know." I walk to the water's edge and start throwing pebbles. I'm not sure I'm capable of doing what he's asking.

"The series your uncle was writing is lucrative."

That was certainly true. I just had a million dollars handed to me.

"Why don't you start the process, and we can see how it goes?"

"What is your role in this whole deal?"

"I was your uncle's agent, and I'd be happy to be yours."

"Would I have to remain anonymous?"

"No, and that might be the perfect angle for the press for the new release. Niece taking over her lost uncle's work. Could give us quite a bump in sales."

"It sounds like you don't need it though."

"We don't, but it won't hurt the brand, that's for sure."

Uncle Don had a whole brand. Have I walked right into a fairy tale? I've been given a house, a sizable bank account, and a job, all on a silver platter.

"I'll send the edits to you. Take a look and see what you think. I guess I should've prefaced all of this by asking: did you like his book you recently read?"

The truth is I did. And I like it even more now knowing that he wrote it.

"Yes, I devoured it."

"Good. Good. This is going to be better than I imagined."

Thomas digs into the details, but I don't absorb most of them other than the fact that Thomas is also J. Edgar. I'm hung up on the fact that that my uncle wrote these books, and I want to know more. Like how close was the heroine modeled after my mom, other than her name? My dad's the only one who can answer that now. Did he dedicate them all to me? I have so many questions and no way to get the answers. I vow to read each book in the series to get more clues. My heart pangs, because it would have been lovely to have discussed so many things with him while he was alive. But now it's my job to bring his legacy to life. I did it with Harvest Fest, and I hope I can do it with this.

Before I look at the edits, I need to read all of his books. I grab the next and bring it back outside to my perch on the deck.

TWENTY-NINE

JOSH

Dave's truck is loaded up with the rented cider press. No one would be brave enough to steal it on the ferry, so Sylviane and I walk up to the quiet room. It's cold out, but the sun heats the room that looks almost like a solarium. We walk in and sit down in one of the twenty plastic seats. It's quiet, like its name, probably because it's empty. I sit down and watch the seabirds fly by as we pull away from the dock. The ferry safety message signals my Pavlovian response, telling me to relax, as Sylviane moves around in her seat next to me.

"I've been keeping something from you," she says.

My pulse quickens from its ferry resting rate. Something like this always happens. Open my stupid black heart a tiny bit and it gets sliced and diced.

"Yeah?" I look straight out toward the horizon and the cargo ship coming into view from the Pacific. Operation Turn On the Hard Exterior has begun.

"I don't want you to think differently about me."

Okay. She's been convicted of a crime. Part of the witness

protection program, had to relocate, and isn't really Don's niece. I shake my head, still staring out at the sea.

"I've recently come into some money."

Robbed a bank. Runs a pyramid scheme selling workout drinks to unsuspecting seniors.

"Interesting," I say. My curiosity piques.

"My uncle left me a lot of money."

Not possible. "Don? He took home packets of ketchup from The Old Owl. He reused paper cups from the Troll."

Sylviane looks away. "Maybe that's part of the reason he had so much money," she says. "He had a secret job."

Sold prescription drugs on the black market. Ran a ring of sex workers.

"He wrote cozy mysteries."

I laugh. A slap-my-knee laugh. "There's no way," I say. If she told me Don was a transcendentalist poet, I might believe it. Literary criticism, possibly. Writer of cozy mysteries, inconceivable.

"I'm serious." She pulls *Secrets of Salty Shadows* out of her tote bag and tells me the incredible story about Don's illustrious career. I hate when people say they're shook, but that's the only word to describe how I feel.

"And I'm taking over the series."

"Let me get this straight. When I met you, you were a magician who'd never crossed the Continental Divide. You calculated the tax before you decided if you could buy something. Now, you're an author of a best-selling series and owner of an apple farm with a large sum of money."

Sylviane blushes. "I know, and I literally have done absolutely nothing to earn any of it. I've paid my way and made it through with so little all my life, and now my cup runneth over. I kind of feel like a fraud."

I get what she's saying. It has to be strange to go to bed

worried about paying for your next meal and waking up able to buy filet mignon. But she deserves this good hand.

"It's your turn to reap the rewards of what you put out in this world."

She grabs my hand, pulls it up to her mouth, and plants a kiss on it.

"I've been so caught up with getting here, planning Harvest Fest, and trying to get everything settled. I've lost a bit of myself. It's been a while since I've relaxed," she admits.

"That's exactly what we're going to do today—play tourist."

"Where to first?" Sylviane looks out across the Sound.

"We're going to check out the Space Needle, and then we'll make our way down to Pike Place and all the sights around there."

"Like to the top of the Space Needle?"

"For sure," I say.

We drive off the ferry and take care of the cider press. The city's better on foot, so we park the truck and walk along the waterfront to grab some fried clams at Ivar's. We eat as we meander up to the Metro. The Metro's a short route from downtown to the Space Needle. It really doesn't make any sense—most of the public transportation in Seattle doesn't.

"It's like a train from Disney!" says Sylviane.

"Never been," I say.

"I went once when I was little. Caroline's gymnastics team was in a competition nearby, so I got to tag along. We did one day at the park and one day sitting in a gymnasium for twelve hours. Anyway, they have a train that looks just like this on a raised platform. It looks just like this."

We get off the train and walk to the Space Needle. Sylviane stops in front of it and just stares.

"This whole place gives off futuristic vibes. Or at least, what people thought the future would look like."

"It was made for the World Fair, so maybe that was on point," I say.

"Let's stand under it," she says.

We walk underneath it. She snaps selfies in all kinds of goofy configurations. She takes one of us from the ground up. After what seems like fifty pictures, she agrees to go up.

The sky's clear today. Mt. Rainier looks majestic and proud. You can see the Olympic Mountains on one side of the Space Needle and the Cascades on the other.

"Where's Greensea?" she asks.

We walk over to the west side, and I point out the ferries going back and forth to the different islands, Greensea just to the north.

"I don't think there's another city in the United States that's this connected via the water. You can be on Greensea and have no idea that this big, vibrant city is a few miles away. You can be on the island and feel like there's nothing around you. It's pretty amazing."

She hasn't stopped smiling all day. She's wearing a long blue-and-yellow sundress under a cream wool sweater with sneakers. I was ready to make her change her shoes if she had flip-flops on again. Her purple messenger bag is slung over her shoulder.

I take a picture of her with Greensea in the background for her Instagram. We sit on the bench outside in the cool sun. Our thighs touch, and I wish we weren't in public.

"This is magical. It's better than I expected up here. I think every newcomer should come up and get this bird's-eye view to understand where they are and the complexity of the area. It's this little carved out place between mountain ranges and bodies of water. There's magic all around us." She takes a deep breath.

When I first got her emails, they annoyed the crap out of me, but now I love hearing her little commentary of everything around us. It gives me fresh eyes, something I've been sorely lacking.

"Want to go to Pike Place Market?" I ask.

"Do you even have to ask? Let's go!"

We take the elevator back down, and I suggest walking since it's mostly downhill and such a rare, gorgeous fall day.

The market's crowded but still has flower vendors lining the walls. Late autumn sunflowers are the mainstay. I buy a bunch and hand them to her.

"Some yellow for you to remember today," I say.

She smiles, a full-tooth smile that moves some of her freckles up on her cheeks.

"They're gorgeous. Thank you."

We walk a little farther in the market.

"What's going on here?" she asks.

"You'll see," I say. We're in a crowd of people gathered around a fish stand. Fishermen clad in yellow overalls are yelling back and forth before they throw fish to each other—gigantic fish to serve a feast.

Sylviane's eyes get big. "Are you kidding? Do they do this all the time?"

"Yep! Can't believe you missed it in your guidebooks!"

"This is so cool. What happens if they miss?"

"They rarely do. But I think they just pick it up and throw it again."

"Amazing."

We grab a bag of mini doughnuts before we head back to the ferry.

"This is the best day." She lands a kiss lightly on my cheek, leaving a trail of cinnamon and sugar.

GREENSEA GAZETTE

Islanders,

Spotted the mapmaker and the magician on the ferry to Seattle, not returning until the late 3:40. Was it a date? Our people say yes, since they were spotted in multiple places holding hands.

Let's have a little lesson on how to drive in a roundabout. The roundabout was not created for you to drive straight through, no matter what type of vehicle you're driving in. Put on your turn signal as you're about to exit. Stop for pedestrians. Yield means yield, and slow down.

The bragging rights as to who created the trendy sport of pickleball have ignited a new island war. An unnamed island wants to take all the credit, but we know the credit belongs to Greensea. The person claiming credit came over here, watched his cousin play this crazy game, and then he took it home to his island. He had more get-up-and-go than his cousin and got all of his friends to play it with him, but it is clear it was created here on Greensea and not anywhere else. I mean, we have Pickles

Harbor! Do we need to say more? The city council has petitioned the state to remove the birthplace of pickleball from the other island, and we hope they'll bestow it here. Good thing old GG has pictures to show Paul playing it in his driveway before they were doing it on that other island.

XOXO,

GG

THIRTY

SYLVIANE

Why does this person want to chronicle my every move? Shit, it's so annoying and intrusive. Finding out who GG might be is my next mission. My desk is covered with the latest entries, and I'm trying to think about who and what I saw around me each time I'm mentioned. The only commonality I think of is seeing Tippy most of the time. But why would she be writing an anonymous gossip column? And wouldn't everyone have figured it out by now?

I google *Greensea Gazette* to find the editors and owners of the paper. Topper Meadowcroft. Meadowcroft. I think that's Tippy's last name too. Facebook's the easiest source of information. There she is—Tippy Meadowcroft. I message her and ask if she knows anything about GG.

I close my laptop and rub my crystals. I can't believe I'm reading stuff like this. Who prints this crap in the paper? It's barely suitable for social media, let alone something published and put into people's mailboxes. I have to put an end to it. A cease and desist won't work because the person isn't using my name. I've learned enough about what's legal to print and what isn't. About three minutes after the Facebook message, my phone rings.

"Hello?"

"Sylviane, it's Tippy."

"Is it you?" I ask.

"Let me start by letting you know that if you ever tell anyone about this conversation, you will completely regret it. I have the power and the ability to make your life a living hell."

"That's a nice way to start a conversation," I say.

"What I'm about to say goes against decades of tradition. No one ever discusses the real GG. And I'm only telling you this because the circumstances are so unusual."

"Okay, Tippy. I will not tell anyone that you and I are having this conversation, but someone is broadcasting my life in the *Gazette* and it's not right."

"Oh, well, that. That was all in good fun."

"So, it is you?"

"It has been me for the last few months."

"Okay, well, you're not doing the greatest job."

"It was your uncle before me," she interrupts.

What in the fresh hell? An anonymous mystery author and an anonymous gossip reporter? For someone who wanted to stay under the radar, why did he pick things that thrust him into the limelight?

"Are you kidding me?"

"Nope."

He had all those piles of papers with lists of names. He must've collected information about people so he had things to write about. It makes so much sense now.

"My father owns the paper. When your uncle passed away, the only way he could think of keeping it going quickly, without revealing it had been your uncle, was to have me do it. I know everyone on the island, so it's easy to have things to write about."

"How long had Uncle Don been doing it?"

"For as long as I can remember. My father and Don go way back. He said the column piqued your uncle's interest early on, so when the previous GG was looking to retire, Don picked it up."

"I haven't seen any emails or anything about it," I say.

"There weren't any emails to his regular email. I think he had a random *Gazette* account, but he typed the columns each week and brought them to my father inside of *New Yorker* magazines. My father gave him a check from the parent company, so it was pretty much on the down low."

"That's a lot of secrecy for a gossip column."

"It's legendary though. It has a long legacy on this island. I believe if you go all the way back, you may find some columns about the infamous card game that sealed the deal on the house you're living in."

That far back, wow. Tippy's being nice to me now, but I'm still compelled to lodge my complaint.

"Do you like what it's become?" I ask.

"I'm new at it. I'm trying to find my rhythm. Give me time. And don't do anything interesting and you'll keep yourself out of there."

"I didn't think I was doing anything of interest, Tippy."

"You're fresh meat." I can practically hear her shrugging over the phone. "That's interesting to everyone."

I'm feeling bold. Maybe it's the fact that I have a career and a house. Whatever it is, I'm over this.

"Be nice or I'm blowing your cover."

"No!" she yells. "You can't tell. It's the only reason the paper is still staying open. If people didn't read GG, no one would ever buy the paper, and we wouldn't have any advertising money floating in. You're a reporter. You know how hard it is to stay afloat in this business."

"Yeah, but you shouldn't be making money off of hurting people." The columns my uncle wrote were snarky, but nothing like what Tippy's turned it into. "I'm not kidding. I have nothing to lose. I'd be happy to let people know."

"Okay, okay. I'll tamp it down. But what? You're going to be my babysitter now?"

"Just don't be mean spirited and you won't have any issues." Come to think of it, she was a pill at Harvest Fest. "Maybe you need to take CBD or something. Find a hobby. Or a date."

"Whatever," Tippy snaps and hangs up.

I look at the typewriter sitting on Uncle Don's bookshelf. He wrote a gossip column too. The multitude of things I didn't know about him is turning out to be great. But I'm not the only one who didn't know everything about him. No one did. And Tippy, her father, and I may be the only ones who ever know he was the author of GG.

THIRTY-ONE

JOSH

I've happily spent so much time with Sylviane this week that I need to get some work done at the store and at my place. The laundry's not going to do itself. And neither is inventory.

My phone buzzes in my pocket. Ever since I got the accidental text from Sylviane, I race to see if she's sent another one.

> Cliff: Hey. Give me a call when you have a minute to talk.

Cliff. Wonder what he wants out there in the Windy City. Cliff and I were both cartography majors in college. Yes, there were more than two of us in the major. We spent all our time together in school. All-you-can-eat baked potato night at Coaches, on Tuesdays after History of Maps class, was our favorite weekly hangout. He's married now and has a kid. Living a different, maybe more grown-up, life on the mainland while I'm stuck on this island.

"Hey, stranger," Cliff answers.

"It's been a minute. How are you and the fam doing?" I ask.

"Dying for a good night's sleep. Baby has colic, and that means he screams all night, every night," answers Cliff.

There aren't any babies yet in the immediate Sherman family—not that we're opposed to them, just haven't had them. I guess Jac and Johnny are closer than any of the rest of us to having kids. If they had a kid, that baby would come out pooping glitter.

"How are things on the island?" Cliff asks.

"Busy," I answer and give him a quick rundown of what I'm up to.

"Dude, you need to get away."

"If only." At least I don't have any Applehill Farm responsibilities anymore.

"Well, that's why I'm calling. I have an opportunity that might be too good for you to resist," he says.

My ears perk up. "Tell me more."

"Got a call from one of my grad school professors at DePaul who needs to go on a midsemester sabbatical for an undetermined amount of time. He called me and asked me to take over for him, and there's no way I can add one more thing to my life. Daphne will kill me if I teach night classes. She practically hands the baby to me as I walk up the stoop every day as it is. I'm too tired to get divorced right now."

"Teaching? What makes you think I'm qualified?"

"The pool of qualified cartographers is small, and to be honest, he was not overly impressed with the pictures of you as a pirate he found when he googled your name, but it's a temporary position. Nonetheless, he checked out your LinkedIn profile and is interested in talking to you. He likes the work you've done mapping earthquakes around the islands in your area."

"Hmm." The wheels turn in my head. I've wanted to leave Greensea for as long as I can remember, but now I hesitate.

"Not sure the timing's quite right for me," I say.

"Dude, opportunities in our field are few and far between. This is a gift. How could the timing not be right? You just listed a dozen menial jobs you're doing on the island. You need this."

"Well, um, I just started dating someone." I'm embarrassed to say it, because Josh Sherman has never let a female come between him and an opportunity.

"This is not forever. At least, I don't think it is," Cliff says.

That's true. It's just temporary, and this thing with Sylviane is so new. I'm not sure if I should make decisions based on it. But until she arrived, I wanted to leave, and now everything seems brighter.

"Be warned, Chicago's not balmy this time of year," says Cliff.

"How bad can it be?"

"Well, if you're headed here in the next few days, it will get pretty cold and windy."

"Isn't the wind just an old wives' tale?" I ask.

"Most old wives' tales are built on at least an inkling of truth, even if that one is more about politician's than weather," Cliff says.

A professor. In Chicago. Best opportunity I've been given maybe ever, but shit, the timing is absolute trash. "I'll talk to him. Give him my number." It's the least I can do.

"Thanks. I'll send you an email with all the deets. You're saving my marriage."

I slump onto my couch. I should pop champagne. I have eight thousand reasons I want to vacate this island, and I've just been handed a ticket off. Yet all I want to do is hike with Ferry Girl.

A professor. Professor Sherman. I could get used to the sound of that. But I'm not sure I want to right now. Because of her my nose perks up when it smells anything remotely resembling cinnamon because I think it might be Sylviane. If I hear someone on a trail, I walk a little faster to catch up in case it's her. I even like the flip-flop noise her ridiculous shoes make. And forget about how she took control and got on top of me in bed. Un-freaking-real.

I've got to talk to someone about this. The family procedure is simple; if something comes up, you text the chat, and then whoever's free jumps on a Zoom. It's early enough that Mom and Dad should still be up.

Ten minutes later, everyone's convened.

"What's up, Josh?" asks Jac.

"Everything okay at the store, Son?" asks Dad.

Mom and Dad look like they're tucked into a dark booth somewhere.

"I'm seriously considering taking a job in Chicago as a professor. It's just temporary, and I'm still working out the details, but it could start soon if it all works out."

"Joshy, that is just the bee's knees," coos Mom.

"Proud of you, Son!" bellows Dad, and the rest of the family echoes their congratulations.

"Finally getting some time off the old island," cheers Ollie.

"What about the girl?" asks Jac.

"Yeah, what about her?" asks Dave, and I can feel the glare he's giving me through the screen of my laptop.

"It's not forever," I say. "And I'm not a hundred percent sure I'll do it."

"Josh, people don't ask twice. You'd be a fool not to take it," says Dad.

A fool. Maybe I'm a fool in love. All the things Sylviane's

shared with me about her childhood: how no one ever hugged her, how Ryder kept leaving her and never returning. There's no doubt this will be a gut punch. There are email and video calls, so many different ways to communicate now, but it's not going to matter when she's sitting in the cabin on her own. And what if something happens? Who's she going to call? Dave?

THIRTY-TWO

SYLVIANE

My Halloween costume started as an ironic joke years ago and I've grown to love it. Everyone in Virginia was familiar with my grungy Cinderella costume. Not the Cinderella going to the ball, the Cinderella who has to sweep the floors. Definitely not a popular choice. In fact, I've never seen anyone else in it. It's a plain gray dress with a brown smock over it and a bandana in my hair. Simple, but effective.

Main Street is closed to cars for the evening and replaced with people. I didn't know this many people live on the island. The cutest little kids walk around trick-or-treating at all the stores, and grown-ups walk up and down with their beverages. Costumes here are creative, a mom's Pinterest dreams: baby pirates, baby sharks, baby geese. I even pass a baby Elton John and an Elvis. A broken-down ferry. A miniature tub of popcorn. A gorilla in a bikini and a pig in a blanket. You can't help but smile.

In the center of town, there's a pyramid of jack-o'-lanterns. Every family who lives on the island must've donated one.

Spooky faces. Happy faces. Dedications to sports teams. Words. Emojis. As many pumpkins as there are costumes. Greensea brought their A game for Halloween. I'm beginning to suspect they bring it to everything they do.

Everyone's smiling and laughing with friends. I see faces I recognize from Harvest Fest, but no one I really know. Josh said he'd be down soon.

An angel taps me on the shoulder and stops me from my people watching.

"Hey there," she says. As if pigs are flying, Tippy's an angel.

"Nice choice of costume," I say.

"Fake it till you make it." She gulps. "Are you Orphan Annie or something?"

"Cinderella, of course."

Tippy lifts her eyebrows and looks me up and down. "You're the only person in the world who picks the depressing version of Cinderella."

"I'll take that as a compliment." I glance around at the street. "This ordeal's pretty amazing."

"Yeah, you get used to these things if you're from here," Tippy says. "Greensea hasn't met a holiday they don't do up to the nines."

We walk down the street a little before we're stopped by a group of teenagers dressed as zombies carrying instruments. They stand in the middle of the street, spanning from sidewalk to sidewalk. A crowd gathers around them, and they play Michael Jackson's "Thriller," complete with dance steps. I'm mesmerized. Their faces are painted white with drips of blood, and they're wearing torn pants and shirts. Until you've seen a kid moonwalk with a tuba, you haven't lived.

"That. Was. Amazing!" I say to Tippy.

"Another Greensea tradition," she says in a ho-hum voice.

"How could anyone ever get bored with this?" I ask.

"Grow up here and you'll see." Tippy's mood doesn't match her costume.

"Hey, Sylviane," says a deep voice with a werewolf mask and a pair of waders.

It can only be Dave. One, because I know it's not Josh, and I don't know anyone other than him; and two, waders, duh.

"What's up, Dave?"

"How'd you know it was me?"

I roll my eyes.

"I'm heading down to the brewery. Want to join me?" he asks.

"Yep, I'm meeting Josh there soon. He's finishing up some work."

Dave lets out a little "hmmph."

I look at Tippy.

"She can come too," he says.

"Thanks. But I need to do some recognizance," says Tippy and walks away.

"Whatever!" yells Dave, and she flaps her wings.

We walk down the street and make our way to Greensea Beers. It looks like an old mechanic's spot right near the ferry. The garage doors are open, and the entry is filled with picnic tables. I grab us a seat and Dave brings me a beer menu. I'm obsessed with the names of things on Greensea. Misty Morn Stout, Pickles Harbor Porter, Greensea Gale Wheat, Gulls Beak Dopplebock. The people of Greensea are committed to original-ity, and I'm here for it.

"What would you like?" asks Dave.

"Golden Hour Pale Ale, please."

"Coming right up."

Costumed people walk by from the ferry. Greensea attracts people from all over.

Dave sets a beer down in front of me, and Josh comes up behind him in an unsurprising pirate costume.

"Hello, Pirate Josh." I smile. He leans down and plants a kiss on my cheek.

"Hello, Ferry Girl," he says. "Or should I say scullery maid?"

"Cinderella." When I wear this costume, I need to remember to put on a name tag. "This is so cute! Virginia had nothing like this. It's out of a movie scene or something," I gush.

"Nothing like a holiday on Greensea," says Dave, and we cheers.

A gorilla in a bikini and a pig in a blanket approach our table and say hello. I'm not in the mood for small talk with strangers, but they sit down on either side of the bench.

"Nice rubbers, bro," says a muffled voice. The costumed creature has an accent I can't quite place.

Dave glares at him. The pig giggles. Dave stares at it. Josh looks at the pig, then back at the gorilla. He squints like he's trying to see through the eye slits of the pig.

"I know that laugh," Josh says, cocking his head to the side.

"Shh!" says the gorilla.

"What the hell are you two doing here?" Josh asks.

"Shh...Keep your voice down," says the pig.

"What? Who are they?" I ask.

"It's Jac and Johnny," Josh says. I feel my cheeks get red. I'm sitting across from The Johnny Nickel, and I'm dressed in a peasant Cinderella costume.

"What the hell are you doing here?" Dave asks this time.

"Shhhh! We wanted to surprise you guys, and Johnny wanted to see what Halloween was like on Greensea."

"But I didn't want all the fanfare. No need to take away from the kids' fun," Johnny adds.

"Introduce us to your friend," says Jac to Josh.

"Sylviane, this pig is my sister, Jac. The gorilla is her boyfriend, Johnny."

"Nice to meet you," I say.

"I thought you had enough of surprise visits," says Josh.

"Johnny's making me change my ways." She giggles.

"You guys want a beer?" Dave asks.

"I'm dying for one, but I need to take this suit off first," says Johnny.

"How about I grab one with a straw for you two?" Dave says.

It's the one day a year no one would think twice about someone drinking a beer with a straw because they're so committed to their costume.

"I'm so happy to meet you!" Jac says and wraps a pig arm around me and Johnny gives a gorilla wave.

I'm frozen. Like I have stage fright. Josh rubs my back and Dave saves me when he comes back with two pints, each with a straw. A few minutes ago I was all alone, and now I'm hanging at a bar with the greatest rockstar of my generation, my boyfriend (I think that's safe to say), and his family.

"Sylviane was about to tell me what she's been up to, before you two interrupted," says Dave.

My life seems inconsequential and small compared to Johnny's. Oh, gee...umm...I write cozy mysteries?

"Been learning more about my uncle," I say.

"Yeah? I loved Don. Interesting guy. Always had a fun fact to share. Whenever I did work for him, he was holed up on his computer," says Dave. "Insurance business must've kept him busy."

I laugh. I've read his latest book, accepted the edits, and signed a contract. I'm not under any obligation to lie. There will be a big press roll out, but I can start by telling them the truth.

"He wasn't an insurance agent," I say.

"Yeah, broker, whatever," says Dave.

"You're never going to believe this," says Josh.

"No, actually, he wrote a twenty-five-book series of cozy mysteries," I say.

"Blimey! I love a good cozy mystery!" says Johnny. "What did he write?"

I give them the lowdown. The brewery is getting crowded, and I can see Johnny looking around, not wanting to be seen.

"Want to do one more lap through town and go back to Mom and Dad's?" asks Jac.

"You okay with that?" Josh asks me.

"Yeah. Sure," I say.

"Do you think Quinn could do up some takeaway for us?" asks Johnny. "I'm starved, and I don't suppose there's much food at your parents' house."

"Good idea. Sylviane and I'll head over there to get some food and meet you all at the house. Dave, text Ollie and tell him the plan," Josh says.

"Are you sure you're okay with this?" he asks me as we walk down the street.

"Absolutely," I say.

"My family can be a lot."

"I'm less worried about your family and more worried about being out with a global mega star. What if I make a fool of myself?"

"Trust me. Johnny is a regular guy, and you'll forget pretty quickly that he's famous at all."

"He's Johnny Nickel! That's almost like saying you'd forget Elvis was famous if you were hanging out with him."

The Old Owl is hopping. Josh makes it easy on Quinn and orders six of the same thing. We sit at the bar and wait.

"How about I leave my car down here and we drive up to my parents' in your car?" asks Josh.

Josh drives Old Blue to the Sherman house.

"Prius, Prius, Tesla," I say, as we drive down the road.

"What are you doing?" he asks.

"It's my version of duck, duck, goose with an island spin on it."

He laughs. I can't really focus on the fact that I'm going to be spending time with his siblings because I'm so wrapped up in the I'm-going-to-meet-Johnny-Nickel situation. They act like it's no big deal, but meeting the guy who's been *People*'s Sexiest Man is kind of huge. And I'm dressed like a peasant.

The scent of pumpkin spice meets my nose as we walk in, and I hear laughter and chatter.

Johnny and Jac have taken off their costumes. Jac greets me first and wraps me in a hug.

"I'm so glad to meet you! I don't know how you've done it, but you've made this guy less grumpy," she says.

I smile. I don't know how I've done it either.

Johnny reaches his hand out and says, "Hi, I'm Johnny Nickel. Pleasure to officially meet you!" Like it really is a pleasure to meet me and not the other way around.

"I'm starved," says Dave, as Josh puts the bags of food on the island. He hands everyone a container and we grab seats around the counter.

"Yo," yells a voice from the garage.

"Olllllie," says Jac, setting down her sandwich and running to the door to wrap the third brother up in a hug.

These guys are tight. It would have been so different to grow up with brothers and sisters and parents who liked me. My face must be showing my distress, because Josh puts a hand on my back and asks me if I'm okay.

"Yeah, you guys are a little too amazing." I take a breath.

"Not what I thought you were going to say," he says.

"So, Sylviane, you inherited Applehill Farm?" asks Ollie.

"Yes, my uncle passed away and left it to me."

"Wow! You must be the fam favorite!" Ollie replies.

More like the only person in the family. Josh and Dave know the full story, and I'm not sure how much to share, so I just say, "Something like that."

But of course a gray answer only begets more questions.

"Is it hard being all the way out here without your family?" asks Johnny in the most amazing British accent.

I forget the lesson I learned early in life, that a pause or silence is more dramatic than words, and I guess I pause too long because Josh has his arm around me and Jac has elbowed Johnny, superstar extraordinaire, who now begins apologizing for asking the question.

"I'm sorry, Sylviane. I didn't mean to ask anything personal," he says.

"It's not your fault. I've just never had this." I gesture to all of them and everything around us. I tend to wear my heart on my sleeve, so I continue. "My mom died in childbirth, and my dad married a woman who was more interested in him than in being my mom. I have a stepsister, but I don't have a family home that's filled with so much joy."

"We will have to change that!" says Jac, and now Josh is glaring at her. "Blah, blah, blah, Josh. She's good for you, and we can be good for her! Even if she dumps your ass, I can still be friends with her."

"I second that," says Dave.

"Here, here," says Johnny.

"Agreed," says Oliver.

When I inherited the house and the money, I knew I was getting things, but possessions can only take you so far. Now, all of a sudden, I'm finding support and love. It's all overwhelming, but I kind of like how it feels. Maybe I'm really building a home.

"How long are you two here for?" Josh asks Jac and Johnny.

"Only until tomorrow," says Jac. "But we'll be here for the holidays."

"Tough life, jetting around on your private plane," says Dave.

"That's not fair!" Jac pushes Dave's shoulder. "You know most of the time I fly commercial."

"Sylviane, have you done much on Greensea yet?" asks Oliver.

"I haven't been here that long, but I have seen quite a bit."

"I've been keeping track of you in the *Gazette*," says Jac. "Man, has that changed lately? I don't know if it was when they outed Johnny or what, but something brought about a big change."

Shit. That would have been Don.

"Even keeping that in mind, it's still more erratic than it was. Like you used to count on waking up and reading GG. Now alerts and updates pop into my email whenever it wants. Twice a day sometimes. Skips a day or two. And it's mean. Like really catty," says Jac.

"Why are you paying such close attention to GG? Isn't your life enough without it?" asks Josh.

"Yes, my life is more than enough, but I like to get the scoop on island life when I'm away." Jac admits.

"I read it too," says Johnny.

Dave smiles. "Johnny Nickel reads *Greensea Gazette*. Who knew?"

"He's like a true islander now. Hey! Let's play a game," says Jac.

Everyone heads toward the family room. I've never played a game with a family. In college, we played games. But I've never played with family members other than the obligatory Candy Land that my dad played with me when I was a toddler. Games seem like a normal occurrence here, especially since

Johnny is the one going to the game cabinet and picking one out.

Turns out this is what I've always dreamed about. Sitting on a family room floor playing Monopoly in teams. Siblings bickering. A familiarity I'm not used to. Josh lets his hand linger on the small of my back, or my knee, making me feel safe. This Halloween is one for the books.

Josh stands up when we finish the game. "I have to get up early and take care of stuff at Cedar & Fern."

"Bet you can't wait till you don't have to do stuff on this island anymore," says Jac.

Josh's head darts back and forth between mine and Jac's. Why wouldn't he have to do things on Greensea anymore? Dave hits Jac's arm, and Johnny rushes up to give me a hug. I feel like there's a conversation taking place without me, but I don't care, because Johnny Nickel is hugging me.

"It was great to meet you guys!" I say as Josh practically pulls me out the door. "What was that all about?" I ask when we get outside.

"Nothing. Just siblings asking how far we've gotten." He rolls his eyes and opens my car door.

The drive to Josh's car is quiet. He seems pensive, and I'm giddy because I just can't wait for the next impromptu game night.

GREENSEA GAZETTE

Islanders,

What a Halloween! We all know who was disguised as a gorilla last night! Can't hide the British accent underneath a furry costume, but nice try. We appreciate the gorilla's continued support of Greensea.

Congrats to all the senior citizens who organized the flash square dance, our official state dance. You give the youngsters an eyeful and something to strive toward! Next year, let's have a dance-off between the thriller zombies and the seniors.

To the teenagers—at least we think they were teenagers—who carved obscene words into pumpkins: we hope the high school comes up with a creative writing assignment for you to properly channel your love of words.

The witches had their annual paddle in Grays Bay. This year, they were joined by a warlock. Please send us pictures if you have any; Ol' GG seemed to miss it!

And lastly, was everyone aghast when they saw the window display at the Greensea Pharmacy? Yes, it was creative, but tampons are not meant to be decorations, especially organic tampons— even if they are the perfect size for miniature ghosts. We're scared to know what they'll use for a display of balloons. The Greensea Downtown Association will issue a new set of guidelines for stores to follow.

XOXO,

GG

THIRTY-THREE

"Sylviane!" Dave is yelling as he runs down the street with a bucket filled with something I can smell before I can see. Dressed in tall rubber boots and a raincoat, he looks like he just walked out of the sea, which he may have, with those creatures.

"Hey," I say. "Oyster delivery?"

"Yeah. How'd you know?" he asks with a smile. "I guess my bucket is a dead giveaway." He looks down at the sea slop. "Bringing them to The Old Owl. Quinn likes to serve them fresh at the bar when she can."

"Nice." I'm not a fan of the slimy things, but I don't want to hurt Dave's feelings, so I'll keep that to myself.

"You doing okay? No more bats?" he asks.

"Nope, it's been great!" Partly because his brother's making me feel like I'm the best thing that's happened to this island since Amazon started delivering over here. "Only bats I saw were on the street last night! If I didn't love Greensea before, I do now."

"Yep, pretty epic night!" says Dave. "What are you up to?"

"Everything looked so cute last night. I just wanted to come down and wander around."

A low damp fog has rolled in off the water, but the sun's trying to burn through. Seagulls chirp and music plays. It's one of those days where I want to pinch myself, because how did this girl who's been alone forever end up with so much in her life? It's like all the dreams I've been scared of have come true. I'm the story with the fairy-tale ending.

I look at the store we're standing in front of, Greensea Gems. A crystal store. My favorite thing, and it's on my island. Things keep getting better and better.

"Ohh! I have to go in here."

"Wait, I'll come in with you."

Dave sets his bucket of sea stuff down and clamors for the door. Long planks of painted white wood stretch out in front of us. Soft harp music emanates from speakers. Glass cases trimmed with driftwood hold every type of crystal. The ceiling's draped with herbs, maybe lavender, and fairy lights. The whole place glows. And smells like cloves and Palo Santo.

"Hey, Meredith," Dave greets the woman behind the counter. "This is Sylviane. She's kind of new to the island."

"Oh, from Applehill Farm! Welcome!"

By now, I'm used to everyone knowing who I am all the time. I mosey around a large round table in the center filled with baskets of crystals categorized by needs.

"What are you looking for today?" asks Meredith.

"Well, I could always use some extra luck and fortitude," I say, even though everything has finally turned around for me.

"Have any rocks that do that?" asks Dave.

"They're called crystals, not rocks, Dave." Meredith rolls her eyes. "I don't call your oysters clams, do I?"

"Point taken."

"How about some amethyst?" Meredith points to some crystals on the counter. "It will bring luck and help with your intuition."

"Who doesn't want that?" asks Dave. "We'll take two." He grabs an old nylon wallet out of his pocket.

"Is that wallet from middle school?" I ask.

"Yeah, what of it?"

I laugh. "I haven't seen one of those since Frankie Collins took me out to Friendly's in eighth grade!"

Dave stares at me. "It was a present from my grandma," he says, taking out the cash. "Meredith, I'm going to need a stone to protect myself from her."

He's Josh's brother, but it's almost like he's mine too. Part of my new instant family.

"Crystal, Dave," says Meredith. "He's a slow learner," she says to me. "And stuck in his ways," she adds, pointing to the wallet.

"Thank you for the crystal. I'll think of you every time something good happens."

"Figured you could use it when Josh heads off."

Wait. I stop in the doorway and look at Dave. What? "Ha-ha! Where's he going?" He would've told me if he were leaving. Maybe Dave doesn't realize how close we've become. Josh has always wanted to leave, but he'd tell me if he were.

Dave looks at me and then reaches down and picks up his bucket.

He's ignoring me. "Wait, Dave. Where's Josh going?"

He looks down the street like he's hoping the sea has risen and it's coming to steal us away. His hesitance is making me worry.

"Dave!" I yell, bringing his attention back to me.

"Nowhere. I mean. You should talk to him." Dave looks to his bucket and holds his hair back with his empty hand. "Shit. He's going to kill me."

"What are you talking about?" Everything's moving in slow motion. I feel the wind lift every single one of my hairs individually. I kind of hear cars moving down the street and the clip-clop of a horse. The stench of Dave's bucket hangs in front of me.

"Nothing. Just don't be mad at him. Promise? He started applying before he knew you," he says and walks away like lightning's about to strike in front of us.

Applying before he met me. For jobs? School? What? My heart's thumping in my ears. Old Blue's down the street, but I might as well have to walk through wet cement to get there. Dave's wrong. I'm sure of it. I reach for the rest of the crystals in my bag and rub them all. I fumble for a quote in the depths of my bag and find a ripped piece of paper I have no recollection of keeping. It says, "Ignorance is bliss." And I want to stand in the ignorant haze of this moment, but I run over to Old Blue and drive as quickly as I can to my new safe haven, the cabin. I wait to call or text Josh because I have this feeling that these are the last few moments of my not knowing.

THIRTY-FOUR

JOSH

When I get back into the office at Cedar & Fern, I've missed six calls from Dave and one from Sylviane. Wonder what's up. It rings again, and it's Sylviane.

"Where are you going?" she asks in a whisper.

"Nowhere. Just finishing up some inventory at Cedar & Fern. I was going to stop by later with a cinnamon roll from Apollo." Since I didn't tell her about Chicago last night, I need to tell her today.

"No. I mean where are you going when you leave Greensea?" she asks in a louder voice.

Oh, shit. I'm too late. "What do you mean?" I'm trying to ascertain what she knows.

"I just saw Dave downtown, and he bought me a crystal that will help me get through when you're gone."

Dave told her? Explains the missed calls. But what the hell?

"I didn't want you to find out this way."

"I don't know what I've found out other than that you're going somewhere."

Shit. Shit. Shit. I should have known that would slip out somehow. I kick myself for not being ahead of the news. I know way better than this. I've had opportunities and chickened out. I never told her.

I take a deep breath and tell her about the job. Her breath is quick, and I swear I hear her sniffling. I can't bear that I'm the one responsible for making her this upset.

"I'm not going," I say as a knee-jerk reaction.

"Why the hell not?" she yells, which is the opposite of what I thought she'd say.

"Not the right time," is all I come up with.

"What does that mean? Does this kind of offer pop up frequently?"

"No, this is the first time."

"Then go."

I can't tell if it's a "Go," but she really means stay, or if it's a "Go, I really mean it." And she hangs up before I can say anything.

I want to see her face, so I can actually have an inkling of how she really feels. I get in the car and head to the cabin. I can make it there in less than five minutes.

The phone rings again.

"Dude! I'm so sorry!"

"What the hell, Dave?"

"You said you were going to tell her last night! I thought she knew," he yells.

"Yeah, I chickened out. I couldn't tell her. She was too happy."

"It's temporary, right?" asks Dave.

"Yeah."

"Then you made it a bigger deal by hiding it from her. Now it's a thing."

He's right. It is all my fault, but I hope when I see her I'll be able to explain myself.

———

The tires of the Prius skid down her gravel driveway, and I run up to the door. When she answers it, she's wrapped up in a black sweater with her arms crossed around her waist.

"I'm sorry," I say, but it doesn't seem adequate. "I just couldn't find the right time to tell you."

Such a lame excuse. She doesn't say anything. We walk into the house and she sits on the couch.

"It all happened so quickly. Want to know the truth?" I ask.

"Um, that should go without saying." She sits back and gets comfortable, letting me believe she's ready to listen. My shoulders relax the tiniest bit, and I sit down next to her.

"Whenever I'm with you, I don't want to go. When we were hanging out with my siblings last night, it all felt so natural. Like you belonged there. Like we belonged there together. That hasn't happened to me before. And I'm not sure I want to leave it, even if it's just for a little while."

"But it's your dream to get off this island." She stares out the big bay window. "Do it."

"I only wanted to get off it when you weren't here. Now that you're here, the place looks a little brighter. I can imagine a future." I sound corny and cheesy. The old me's almost choking on my words.

"I don't want to be responsible for you staying here and missing out on a dream." She stares at me.

"You wouldn't be. It's my decision."

"That's not how it works; you know that. In a couple of months, when I'm not so sparkly, you'll see an ad for Chicago deep dish pizza, and your heart will pang. I'm not going to be the person responsible for that pang. For giving you a what if."

She pushes her sleeve up and starts tracing on her arm. I reach my hand over and try to add some comfort.

She shakes her head no and moves her arm in toward her stomach. "Not right now. How long is this assignment for?"

"That's a little vague. I know I'll be home for the holidays, but it's not clear if he'll need me next semester." I muster as much enthusiasm as I can.

"And then you're coming back?"

"That's the plan. This was not something I was looking for. It came to me," I remind her.

"You don't owe me an explanation." She still plays with her sleeve. "It's not like we're together."

I cock my head to the side and squint my eyes. We kind of are together. Or at least, we got together. This could go one of two ways. It's a pivotal moment in our maybe non-relationship. I stare up at the log ceiling. There's no denying that my life is better when she's around. And at this early stage in our unclassi-fied thing, leaving will have a profound impact.

"Are you saying you don't want there to be anything between us?" I ask.

"If you're going to Chicago, it's hard to have a relationship. I'm just getting to know Greensea, and now you're leaving."

"Temporarily," I remind her. "If I were staying, would there be something?"

"Yeah, maybe. I mean, behind your grumpy attitude there are a few redeeming qualities." She raises her lips in a half smile.

"Every time I've been grumpy, it's been because someone deserved my attitude," I defend.

She rolls her eyes. Which I probably deserve.

"Do you want to take a pause?" I ask, not really sure what to say next.

"A pause? Look, Ryder and I had a strange relationship, and he jerked me around all the time. I'm not interested in that." She pulls her sleeve down and crosses her arms again.

"I have no intention of 'jerking you around.'" I use air quotes.

"He came and went on his terms. I had no idea what he was doing when he wasn't with me."

"This doesn't have to be like that. If we decide this is a thing, I'm not going to leave you hanging. I'm not going to go to Chicago and hook up with someone else." I put my hands into my pockets instead of doing what I want to do, which is reach out and touch her.

She twirls her hair around her finger.

"I'm not Ryder. I don't do things on the side."

She half smiles. "Your eyebrows are twitching."

"Glad at least part of me could amuse you."

"When does this thing start?"

I'm afraid to tell her because this may be the worst part.

"I leave the day after tomorrow."

"Wow. Okay, let's take a break." She walks to the front door and opens it. I take it as my cue. I reach in to give her a kiss. She takes a step back. My shoulders slump down five inches.

We'll take a break. But that's the last thing I wanted to hear.

THIRTY-FIVE

SYLVIANE

The rain began the moment he left. I wanted to text him, to call him, to stop by the store. But I resisted. I knew he'd stay if I'd shown any weakness, or any desire. What's that old quote about setting free the one you love? That's what I had to do. If it's meant to be, he'll come back. I hope.

Unless Josh is like Ryder. When Ryder left the first time, I didn't realize what was going on. We'd gone on a couple of dates, and then he ghosted me, only to show up at my apartment three weeks later like nothing happened. Then he took me out to dinner at the best ramen spot in the area. Treated me to a private showing of *Breakfast at Tiffany's*. Got tickets to a sold-out speaking engagement by my favorite author. Wowed me with his intense listening skills and attention to detail. And then disappeared for a few more weeks. Each time he came back, I welcomed him with open arms (and legs). He was like the perfect piece of cheesecake. I gorged myself on being with him when he was around, felt sick when he wasn't, and jumped right back in when he was in front of me.

I couldn't let things be the same with Josh. And I never thought the universe would throw the same twist again. I needed to close up my heart, not think about his crusty exterior and cream puff filling. His loyalty to my dead uncle. He does the right thing, all the time. And his eyebrows. His lips. Oh, and his fingers.

Josh texted to say goodbye and to say he was taking an early ferry to the airport. When I got up, I found a pair of hiking boots on my doorstep with yellow laces and filled with quotes. I haven't taken them off since. I piled the quotes into one of Uncle Don's mason jars. From what I've seen so far, they range from funny, to ridiculous, to classic, to modern. I knew my love language revolved around words, but words inside appropriate footwear...Take me to bed or lose me forever. Except he can't, because he's gone.

I walk on the ferry with a hundred other people. It's drizzly and cold, but I still like to look out the window, even if it's hard to see through the windblown raindrops. Turns out my favorite spot on the ferry is a booth near the galley, just where I saw Ferry Guy sitting the first day we unknowingly met. I'm close enough to the food and far enough away from the restrooms that I don't have to hear the constant flushing of toilets.

I curl up in my booth and lean my head against the window. It's like the heavens are crying my tears. Somehow, I lose everyone. Over and over again. They (who are they, anyway?) say you receive lessons until you learn them. What else do I need to learn? I think I've handled it well thus far. It exhausts me though, because I want someone to be with me, like all the time. I want to cringe at his morning breath. Try to make something from the ingredients in the fridge. Garden together. I want to do the everyday chores that are better when someone's with you.

I told him to go, and I appreciate that he wanted to stay and struggled with his decision, but I just hope he comes back.

I call Beth from the ferry so she can help me make sense of it all.

"He's moving away. Temporarily, but still not going to be living on the island for a while," I tell her.

"So? Do you like him?" she asks.

"Yeah, I actually do." I think about it, and I know I'm ready for it. "I want all the swoony things."

"Girl, I do not know how this world has not beaten it out of you already, but you deserve it more than anyone I know." It's like she's trying to send me a giant hug through the phone.

"Yeah, well, I thought my luck had changed. Look at everything that's happened to me lately! But then he left, and it's the same old thing again."

"It doesn't sound like it. He's not Ryder. He'll be back."

I wonder what's giving her crystal ball faith in him, but the call drops as we reach the middle of the Sound.

The message comes on, reminding us to disembark the ferry in the vehicle you arrived on. I want to stay and just ride back. The slow rock of the waves soothes my soul. A crew member walks by, so I ask.

"Hey, is it okay if I stay on and ride back?"

"No, ma'am. State law requires you to get off and get back on."

I pick myself up and walk down the glass-enclosed walkway, bracing myself for the wet cold when I get outside. It's only about thirty steps to enter the terminal and then get back in line, but they're a damp thirty steps.

On my second ride, all hell breaks loose when a little girl accidentally frees her brand new pet gerbil, and ferry riders rush to help capture it. A lady with a leather bucket bag opens it up on the floor and the gerbil scampers in. At least the incident takes my mind off my crumbling heart.

By my third ferry ride, a worker in the galley takes pity on me and lets me stand behind the cash register, so they don't make me get off again.

On my fourth ride, someone comes up behind me.

"Get off the boat, Syl," says Tippy.

"What are you doing here?" I ask.

"I was in the city for the day and got a hot tip that you were riding back and forth like a lovesick puppy."

She looks me up and down. I definitely fit the description. Meanwhile, she's wearing a camel trench coat and carrying a leather briefcase, like she's come from an actual professional meeting.

"Pull it together, DuPont. You're a strong woman. You're made of stronger stuff than this. You going to fall to pieces every time a guy leaves you?"

I don't answer.

"No! You're not. You're going to give yourself a few minutes of wallowing, eat one of Apollo's cinnamon rolls, and make a life for yourself. Rumor has it a book's coming out soon."

How does she know about that? Is she tracking my email? Hanging out at my mailbox?

She goes on. "You have a property that needs your attention. And I need a friend."

I humph at this. "First, how do you know evvvverrrything that goes on on this island, even when it happens behind closed doors?"

"Not giving away my secrets. But I have moles all over the place. You'd be surprised what happens in the back room of the post office. Or in the safe at the bank."

I shake my head. I do not want to know how Tippy's curried everyone's favor.

"Second, why do you think I'm going to be your friend?"

"Because you don't have anyone else. You don't have a choice."

Not one piece of her hair's astray. I'm not sure how she walked on this ferry and managed to maintain this look.

"Maybe I don't want a friend. I thrive on being alone."

"Everyone wants a friend like me," she says, and puts her arm through mine. "Even you."

"Will you keep me out of GG? Wait. Let me rephrase that. You'll keep me out of GG."

"How about I'll just be nice?"

I can tell by her tone it's a rhetorical question.

We dock and Tippy walks me off the ferry and deposits me at Old Blue. "You done with your pathetic displays of desperation?" she asks.

I know my answer doesn't even matter, but I say yes anyway.

Tippy looks me in the eye. "You need to learn. Not everything you love leaves for good. The right things come back to stay." She starts to walk away. "Keep being your own heroine, Sylviane. Don't let this new chapter be defined by what you've lost."

Wow. Wise words from Tippy. I needed to wallow. To lose myself in the waves. Now, I'll go get that cinnamon roll...and hope.

GREENSEA GAZETTE

Dear Islanders,

Have no fear, dear readers! The tale of the mapmaker and the magician is hardly over. Even though he's spending his days in a blustery city, it's hard to imagine he'll find anyone better.

Did you see that sunrise? Waking up to a cotton candy sky is a great way to start the day.

Miss Nelson's first graders delivered cards to the senior living community. Is there anything cuter than kids and old people? Of course there isn't.

Election Day is complete and the results are in! Mayor Nickerbottom has been reelected, although Barry the Elk had a strong write-in presence.

Kudos to the person who started the petition to ban BMWs on the ferry. We're sorry the council didn't see fit to add it. If you can't secure your car alarm, your riding privileges should be revoked.

The resolution to reroute traffic during newt migration season has been tabled until scientists can offer more proof that cars are responsible for a decrease in the population. Leave it to Greensea, we're always trying to save something!

XOXO,

GG

THIRTY-SIX

JOSH

When I left for Chicago, it felt like things were over, even though we had just called it a break. But I decided within minutes of landing in the Windy City that I wanted to push us forward during our pause. Sylviane was the cheese on top of my burger that I didn't know I needed. So I started sending emails, hoping we'd get back to our easy repartee.

To: sdp@email.com
From: jmatey@email.com
Subj: Thoughts from the Windy City

S.,

Picked up the curriculum for the remainder of the term. Should be easy. My apartment's barely bigger than the one over the store. It's on the

corner of two busy streets, in between the bus
route and the elevated train they call the El.
Between the double modes of transportation, it's
easy to get anywhere anytime of day or night, but
it's loud with trains going by every few minutes.
My view of Jewel-Osco's fluorescent 24-hour sign is
somehow not as peaceful as my partial view of the
Sound on Greensea. And Chicago doesn't have as
many trees.

J.

I wished email had three little dots like a text message. At least
I'd know she was typing.

Chicago's a city. Greensea's a floating forest.
S.

The replies were slow at first, but I didn't want to give up. I
knew I could crack her.

S.,

Went to the top of the Hancock Tower today. Felt
like the entire thing was going to blow over. I
wanted to see the lake from above, and what they
say is true—it feels just like an ocean. I know it's a
Great Lake, but I didn't expect it to feel as large as
it does. Headed over to the Billy Goat Tavern after-

**ward for a cheeseburger. I'm like the tourist extra-
ordinaire. I think you'd be proud.**

J.

Waiting for a response was akin to waiting to open presents on
Christmas morning.

Have pizza yet?
S.

A question had to be a good sign.

S.,

**Yes! I'm trying to figure out which is better—Gior-
dano's or Gino's East. Seems everyone has their
opinion. I'm torn. I like the cheese-sauce ratio of
Giordano's better and the crust of Gino's East.
Which did you like when you were here? Good ol'
Greensea Pies could learn a thing or two from
them, it seems.**

What have you been up to?

J.

I had to wait twenty-four hours to get a reply. It felt like three weeks.

Been working on the edits for the book. It's more work than I thought it would be. I've spent a lot of time wandering around the island with Tippy, trying to get into the main character.
S.

That's not what I expected her to say.

Tippy?

J.

Yep. Believe it or not, she's been a good friend to me.
S.

It's hard to believe, but I guess anything's possible. Our emails continued with daily updates for the rest of my time in Chicago.

I had imagined a big lecture hall inside of a brick building with columns. Leaves turning color on the trees. Students walking around with backpacks and barn jackets. But my class, Introduction to Mapmaking, was housed in a strip mall three quarters of a mile from the main campus, next to a sandwich shop that must specialize in Italian seasonings, because the smell of them was pouring out of every vent, leaving my six students and me starving. Lecture halls are reserved for the big dogs; satellite classrooms are for majors that don't bring in a lot of money, and cartography fits that bill.

A typical class period: one student's asleep. Another's openly vaping. One appears to be older than I am. The other three are on their phones, "recording" the lecture. Not exactly what I was hoping for.

I open my notes and begin my last ninety-minute lecture, putting myself to sleep as well as the students. I worked out a deal with the dean, so my last few lectures after Thanksgiving could be virtual. This will be my last one in person, and I can go back to Greensea, and Sylviane.

Every minute that I wasn't teaching in the mall, I walked the city. I've been averaging ten miles a day. I've seen every building in Lincoln Park, the zoo, the lake, Wrigley. It's like Ferris Bueller is my tour guide. But I miss the trees, and the marine air. The foghorns. Even the *Gazette*. And I miss my Ferry Girl.

I wished to leave the island for so long, always thinking the grass was greener off the "rock." But now I've had my adventure off the island, and the only word that can describe it is gray, and well, oregano. Life on Greensea is in technicolor. Not just because of the water and the trees. It's the people too. Life in a city carries anonymity, which on one hand is luxurious and on the other is soul crushing. It'd be easy to die alone.

I can't wait to see the mountain as I land at SeaTac, get on the ferry, and surprise Sylviane.

THIRTY-SEVEN

SYLVIANE

Dad and Nancy come tomorrow, and I'm in a total panic. My Greensea life and my old life are going to collide, and I do not want Nancy to wreck anything here. Her judgmental ways may cloud my vision, or she might piss people off and put me on the Greensea Naughty list. To top it off, it's the first time I've ever hosted a holiday, and I feel like one of those instant pots that needs to let out all the steam. I ordered a precooked meal from Quinn, but I still feel obligated to cook something, like a pie. Between finishing the book edits and getting the guest room sorted for them, I've barely had time to think about missing Josh or to respond to his emails. It's made the days easier, but I'd be lying if I said I didn't miss the smell of his leather jacket or the stomp of his Doc Martens.

Today's agenda is all about finishing touches. A plant in the guest room. Stock the fridge with strawberry-banana yogurt (Dad's favorite) and hazelnut creamer (a Nancy necessity). A candle that's not too perfumey (must smell like an actual thing, like pine trees or sage, not a rainy morning). Soap that smells like fresh linens. Basically things Nancy can't complain about.

Sunshine's Flowers is filled with people picking up Thanksgiving table centerpieces, something I never contemplated. I pick up a tiny Christmas cactus that will look nice on the bedside table and might even bloom while they're here. Sunshine has a display of soaps. I give several the scent test and pick up one that should fit Nancy's needs.

The drive from Sunshine's to the candle shop is short, but traffic's at a standstill. How can there be a traffic jam on this island? The guy a couple of cars ahead of me gets out and walks down the road. Then the next person does the same, and the next. Great. Now when traffic starts to move, I'll still be stuck because they're not in their cars. But we don't move, and there aren't any cars coming in the opposite lane. Shit. I hope no one's hurt. My heart seizes a little when I realize I should send good thoughts into the universe instead of complaining about people leaving their cars. As soon as I have that thought, I see a gang of people running in my direction. It's not until they're two cars away that I see they're running after a little black and white pig that's zig-zagging its way down the road. Traffic remains at a standstill, most of the drivers are chasing the pig, and I'm not sure when it will start again. But I have to admit, the little pig is adorable.

Eventually, three people come from behind and I roll down Old Blue's window to ask if they caught the pig.

"Hey, Sylviane!" says a guy I've never seen before. "Yeah, Victor lured it into the station wagon back there. The little porker isn't too happy, but at least it's contained and didn't get hit." I look in my rearview mirror and see people standing around a brown Subaru, passing things through a slit in the window. Everyone ambles back to their cars, and traffic crawls down the road.

I run into the little shop on Main Street that has all the scented candles and find the most basic fir candle I can. Mindy tries to sell me Sunrise on a November Morn, but I know that's just the kind of thing that Nancy will hate, and we'll have to hear her go on and on about the meaning behind the name, what she thinks the candle actually smells like, and something more appropriate to call it.

From there I walk to Island Grocers, and it is packed. Every household on Greensea must have at least one person at the grocery store doing all of their shopping for the holiday. There aren't any carts left, so I grab a basket and head toward the yogurt. It's clear everyone on the island needs yogurt too, because the selection is rubbish. I grab raspberry vanilla, get the creamer, and head home before I experience any more of Greensea.

———

Shit. The ferry's full, so we have to sit and wait in the parking lot until the next boat comes. Sitting in Old Blue with Dad and Nancy is not a treat.

"So you're telling me anytime you want to go to the city, you have to wait for this god forsaken boat?" Nancy asks, wiping invisible crumbs off her perfect black travel pants.

"Yes, Nancy. It's an island. The only way off and on is by ferry." Unless, of course, you're one of the lucky few who have a seaplane. "And it's the day before Thanksgiving, so it's even busier than usual."

"It's a bit stuffy in here. Turn on the air," commands Nancy.

"This is a no-idle zone. I can't turn the air on," I answer. Not to mention it's November and not what I would call warm.

"Well, roll down the window a smidge," she grunts.

The parking lot is full of rows of cars. As you open the

window, you might as well be sitting in someone else's car. You can hear every conversation. Which normally is fine. But today, there's a couple in a VW bus one row over and two cars ahead of us who are arguing about how much time his mother should spend at their house. And it's not going well. Apparently, he smokes too much weed when his mother's around so he can cope. According to his wife, that's why his mother shouldn't stay so long. He suggests that maybe his wife should find a coping mechanism. The last thing we hear as she climbs out of the bus and slams the door is, "I do! I leave!"

"Dear me. Can't they be quiet?" asks Nancy.

I learned decades ago there was no real reason to answer or acknowledge every question or statement made by Nancy. She likes to hear herself talk, and it's probably why she gets along so well with my dad. He's a quiet pushover. I wonder again if he's always been a pushover or if he became that way when he was a desperate single dad trying to raise a toddler on his own.

"Feel free to get out and walk along the water," I say, hoping she'll take me up on it

"I'm fine. Another hour sitting won't kill me," she says.

It's a gray day, and there are whitecaps on the Sound. The only predictable thing about the fall weather has been the color of the sky. I've never been on the ferry when it's been this choppy, and we might be in for a wild ride.

When we finally load onto the ferry, little waves crash about the bow, and the boat rocks even though it's large.

"I think I'm going to be sick," croaks Nancy.

"Look at the horizon," says my dad.

"I can't! It keeps moving."

"Maybe you'd feel better if you got out of the car," I suggest.

Dad gets out and opens Nancy's door. They walk to the side of the boat, and it must not help, because soon enough she's leaning over the edge and throwing up. I hear a kid a few cars back yell, "Gross!"

While they're occupied with seasickness, I run up to the galley for some ferry wine. I'll be done and back in the car before they even miss me. The boat's crowded with travelers for the holiday. I get in line in the galley and scroll through Instagram while I wait my turn.

"What can I get you?" asks the lady behind the cash register.

"May I have a glass of white wine, please?"

"Chardonnay or Sav Blanc?"

There's a choice? I shouldn't be that surprised.

"Umm...What kind of Chardonnay is it?"

"It's an unoaked wine with a crisp aftertaste, made on the island but from grapes grown in Eastern Washington."

Man, everyone's got their descriptions down.

"Hmmm..." The line behind me is growing, so I resist the urge to ask about the Sav Blanc. "I'll try the Chardonnay, please."

The ferry galley has more choices than some grocery stores. Granted, this cup of wine will probably cost as much as some bottles. I tap my credit card on the pad and pick up my generous pour.

"Excuse me," a voice I recognize says from behind. "Would you like some tater tots with your wine?"

"Josh! What are you doing here?" I almost spill my wine when I see him.

"Finished early. Thought I'd surprise you." He sets the tater tots down on the counter and leans in for a kiss. There's a sigh, a huff, a cleared throat, and an "ahh" in line behind us.

"Sir, would you like to purchase those tater tots?" asks the cashier.

Josh pays for the tater tots, and we walk out to one of the

Formica tables. He's back. I've kept myself occupied and haven't really thought about what it'd be like when I saw him. But now, with him right in front of me, I'm elated and feel like my shoulders just dropped two inches.

"But how'd you know I was on the ferry?"

"Fate." He grins. "Saw you walk into the galley. I planned on showing up at the house; instead you got me earlier."

I take a sip of wine. "This stuff is good!"

"Did you think we were lying about that?"

I laugh and take a tater tot. Josh is here. And I have ferry wine. Life is good. Except I hear a throat clear behind me. Nancy and Dad have found the galley.

"Up here having a glass of wine while I'm seasick downstairs?" asks Nancy.

I ignore her. "Dad, Nancy, I want you to meet my friend, Josh."

Dad reaches his hand out. Josh looks to me.

"They're here for Thanksgiving."

Josh nods and extends his hand to Nancy. "So nice to meet both of you. Sylviane's told me so much about you."

Nancy glares at me, and I know she's afraid of what I've said. "Well, we know nothing of you, but that's no surprise."

"Josh just did a stint as a professor in Chicago." I hope that will at least impress Nancy.

Josh looks at me and smiles. "I hope you can all meet us at The Old Owl tonight. My whole family will be there."

"Everyone?" I wonder if it includes the rockstar.

"Everyone. Come by around seven?"

I nod my head and gulp my wine as fast as I can. The ferry's pulling in, and it's time to get back in the car.

He came back. Before he was supposed to.

Old Man Jackson is clogging Main Street with his buggy

when we get off the ferry. Instead of cute and quaint, Nancy thinks it's a safety hazard to be stuck behind a horse.

I spent the last week turning the basement into a guestroom. I got a bed, nightstands, and an armchair on Buy Nothing Greensea. I ordered new sheets and blankets and turned it into a formidable room. Although it's the bottom floor of the house, there are big French doors with a view to the water. When we walk into the cabin, Nancy doesn't say anything and only makes a few "hmm" noises.

"Where are we staying?" she asks.

"Right downstairs," I say.

"You're putting us in the basement?" she asks, with her hands on her hips.

"It's not really a basement. You'll see." Pleasing Nancy isn't in my wheelhouse, so I just move on.

"I think I'll have a lie down before we go out tonight."

Music to my ears. Dad and I walk down to the water while Nancy stays in and rests.

"Your mom would love that you live here now," he says.

He never spoke about Mom much. Whenever he did, it seemed like he was having stitches removed—every word pained him.

"I like it here," I tell him. "I'm pretty sure Uncle Don used Mom as the main character of his books."

"Oh, that sounds just like him."

There's a treasure trove of knowledge I haven't learned about all of these people, but asking the right questions to get the right answers always evades me.

"Can you tell me about her? What was she like?"

"Well, she was just about your age when she died. And from what I see of how you're living your life now, you're just like her. A real ballbuster."

"I don't know if I'd call myself a ballbuster, Dad."

"Well, you've certainly found your voice since you moved out here. I suppose you felt muffled back in Virginia. And I probably have a lot of apologizing to do for that."

Life would have been different if my dad had been my voice when I needed one, if he had said no to any of Nancy's ideas about what was best for me, but there's no point on dwelling on that now.

"No, you did the best you could." I grab his hand as we walk back up toward the house. "Tell me more about her."

"Oh, Syl. She was magical. You know that thing you do with your nose when you don't like something? You sort of crinkle it up. She did the same thing. The way you stubbornly never give up, like when you tried to juggle oranges for hours on end—got that from her."

The rain picks up and we go inside.

———

The sign on the door of The Old Owl says closed, but Josh comes out the door as we pull up.

"Closed it down just for family tonight," he says.

"Happy Thanksgiving!" says someone who must be Josh's mom. She wraps me up in a hug. Josh holds his hand on my lower back, protecting me from anything that's about to happen. Jac rushes up to me and wraps me up.

"I'm so glad you didn't dump him after he left!" Her cheeks match the fizzy red drink she's holding. Johnny comes up behind her and pats me on the back.

"So glad to have an outsider at these things with me!" He reaches his hand out to shake my dad's hand.

Nancy looks at me. Of course, she recognizes him right away. She's starstruck and wipes her palms on her pants. I've never seen her rendered speechless. But Johnny's a pro, and he hugs her and takes her to the bar for a glass of wine. She looks back at my dad and gives him a shrug and a tiny smile.

Josh whispers, "I gave him the lowdown. He's going to give her the star treatment to keep her happy."

I meet Josh's dad, and the dads head off in search of whiskey. It's like I've been a part of this family for years, the way they've welcomed us. Quinn has a couple of tables set for us with nice tablecloths. She must be trying to impress the rockstar. I hear my dad laugh, a sound I haven't heard in a while. And then I hear him tell Josh's dad that he wants to show him a trick. He walks toward the table, and I know he's about to pull the tablecloth off, so I nudge Josh, and we walk out to the deck and stand under a heater.

"I missed you, Ferry Girl." He steps in for a kiss, and this time I don't have my hands full, so I wrap them around his waist.

"I missed you too, Ferry Guy."

Dear Islanders,

Congratulations! Only one turkey fryer incident on the island yesterday, as far as we know! The Welsh's fryer exploded and landed upright in the Bay. A quick-thinking fly fisherman was able to lasso a rope around it and pull it back in. Word from the Welsh house is that Grays Bay saltwater is the perfect brine. Not an accident, but now a viral TikTok, as their oldest son filmed the whole episode.

Huzzah! The Sherman Family is on the same continent and has been reunited. Rumor has it they had dinner at The Old Owl last night, complete with magic tricks. Wonder what kind of trouble they'll be up to next?

As we approach this holiday season, remember that no matter what type of cup your neighbor carries, recyclable or Styrofoam, they carry stories in their hearts greater than the coffee.

Let us continue to rejoice in the joy of the holidays throughout the year, whether or not it is all that we imagined. Go to the celebrations. Pet the animals at the llama farm. Have that drink with a new friend. Be gracious and festive, island neighbors. Give what you didn't expect to find a chance.

XOXO,

GG

EPILOGUE

June – the last weekend of Local Season

SYLVIANE

Sitting in the cabin having someone do my makeup for my book launch feels surreal. Jac worked her magic and found someone through Johnny's connections to come over to Greensea and help me get all gussied up. They even picked out my clothes, but to be honest, I feel more like the emperor without any clothes. It's like my life is out there for everyone to devour and explore. Sometimes I understand why Uncle Don kept this whole career under wraps. But "Freedom lies in being bold" is the Robert Frost quote I picked out this morning, and it seems to fit for what lies ahead of me.

Josh peeks upstairs to see if it's safe for him to come up and change before we leave.

"My turn?"

The woman doing my makeup brushes powder all over me, takes my cape off, and pronounces me done.

"Your turn." I give my dress a princess twirl. Today, I'm in a green sundress with a fitted top and flowy skirt with pockets for my crystals. A perfect representation of Greensea.

Josh walks up and leans in to give me a kiss.

"No!" the makeup artist yells. "Don't touch her face with any part of yourself."

Josh puts his hands up and backs away. "Okay, okay. Don't worry." Josh looks at me. "Just know I want to, but it will have to wait until after." He gives me a look and heads toward the closet for his clothes.

Josh started spending so much time at the farm with me, it seemed natural for him to just move in. The commute to Cedar & Fern is longer, but ever since his stint in Chicago, he's been doing more work as a guest lecturer at colleges and universities around Seattle and spending less time at the store. With his parents back on the island, they've picked up the slack since, much to their dismay, their RV is backordered.

Josh steps out in a pair of black jeans, Doc Martens, and his leather jacket. Quintessential Ferry Guy, and I couldn't be happier.

The story of Uncle Don writing his series for his deceased sister, and my continuing it, has made national news. I've done spots on *The Today Show*, *Good Morning America*, and *CNN*. Mayor Nickerbottom practically begged me to have my publication day event on the island. Between the Covers is standing room only. There's a gigantic bouquet of balloons on a sandwich board announcing the reading in front of the store. Performing magic tricks in front of kids and their parents is easy, but reading to all these people is another story. I take a deep breath, rub the malachite necklace Meredith made for me, and walk toward the podium.

I didn't know my mom, and I didn't know my Uncle Don very well. A year ago, I thought the history, the stories, the family traditions were lost and something I could never recover. When I found out my uncle was the illustrious author of twenty-five, now to be twenty-six, cozy mysteries, I scoured them for details to map out my family tree. The pages contained a treasure trove of information. I found my great grandma's apricot bread recipe that the Hamiltons had every Christmas morning. I learned my mom was a champion high school debater, my uncle an avid chess player. My uncle preserved their lives in his pages, giving me the greatest gift I've ever been given.

A single tear falls down my cheek. Tippy "humph"s and hands me a tissue. Dad sniffs in the front row. Nancy elbows him. Johnny Nickel and Jac squeeze hands. Dave gives me a thumbs up. I catch Josh's eye, and his lips turn up into a smile and he mouths, "You're doing great." He gives me his trademark sideways smirk that makes me sweat a little and giggle before I continue.

Puzzle at Pickles Harbor *was his last love letter to this island.*

And I read the first two pages of book number twenty-six.

Dear Islanders,

What a lovely book launch for Sylviane DuPont! You all helped put Greensea's best face forward, except, of course, the harebrain who purchased balloons for the event and let them go. Greensea has an ordinance that clearly states no balloon is to be released for any purpose. By our count, there were twelve balloons. That means at least twelve sea animals could have been injured by random pieces of latex falling into the Sound. We assume the author meant no ill intent; she'll claim she's still a newcomer and didn't know the rules, or better yet, didn't know there would be balloons, but we know "someone" is to blame.

We are all thrilled to see love blooming once again in the Sherman family! The mapmaker and the magician seem to have abracadabra-ed themselves into cohabitation.

While on the subject of the Shermans, they've brought a great deal of attention to our fair island, between the song "Greensea Gal" and the publication of the new cozy mystery Puzzle at Pickles Harbor. Good thing there are two more single Sherman brothers...can't wait to see what trouble they get into!

XOXO,

GG

THANKS FOR READING!

Let's keep in touch...

ACKNOWLEDGMENTS

It means so much to me that you chose to spend time on Greensea with the Sherman family. I wanted to create a series that gave off the same small town vibes and comfort I find in watching and re-watching Gilmore Girls. I can't wait to share all the Greensea Island Adventures with you.

The idea for this book, a love story between a mapmaker and a magician, began almost eleven years ago. To see it come to fruition and have people enjoy this story, is a dream come true.

The support I've received for my Greensea books is beyond anything I could have imagined. A huge thank you to the independent bookstores and the small businesses that have purchased copies and asked me to do events.

Thanks to Amberly at Watermark Writing Company for her amazing editing skills and vast knowledge of Gilmore Girls. I'm so glad Jen and I walked into Watermark Book Company!

Thank you to my mom and Gill for being the best proofreaders around! No matter how little time I give each of you, you come through and I genuinely appreciate it!

Thanks to Serena Bell for all the words of wisdom.

Thanks to Jen for being a true partner in this endeavor. None of this would be possible without you...'literally' none of it. Everyone can see your artwork that welcomes readers to Greensea, but they don't see the countless texts, the 24 hour support, the witty one liners, and the endless ideas that you provide. Thank you from the bottom of my heart for helping me make my dreams come true. Can't wait for our next 'research' adventure!

I'm lucky enough to have the support of many amazing women. Whether I'm in a PTSO meeting, watching a lacrosse game, working out on a reformer, or sitting in my pajamas on the deck with my journal...you all lift me up and I can only hope I can return the favor to each one of you someday.

So much gratitude for the friends who send texts to check in and support me no matter where they are in their lives. It means the world!

Thank you to Alex (and Pauline!), Eva, Gigi, and Ethan for supporting my dream. And thanks to Justin for reading and supporting me in more ways than I thought possible.

ABOUT THE AUTHOR

Julie Farley loves writing books filled with big families, lots of heart, and plenty of laughs. She lives in the Pacific Northwest with her husband and four amazing kids. Julie has a bachelor's degree from the University of Notre Dame and a graduate degree from DePaul University. When she's not busy with her family or writing books, you'll find her watching reality TV...of any sort!

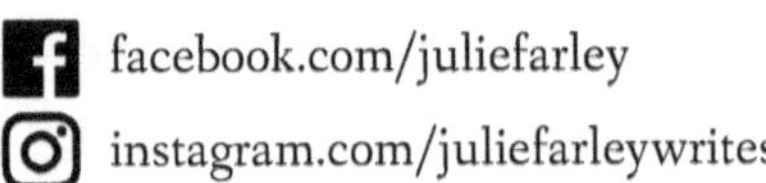

facebook.com/juliefarley

instagram.com/juliefarleywrites

ALSO BY JULIE FARLEY

Love Songs and Ferry Tales

Tripped Up Love

The New Ever After

Another Tomorrow